Punk Faction

Copyright © 2011 by Marcus Blakeston. All rights reserved.

http://marcusblakeston.wordpress.com
marcus.blakeston@gmail.com

This is a work of fiction. Names, characters, businesses, places, events, and incidents are the product of the author's imagination. Any resemblance to actual persons, living or dead, events, or places is entirely coincidental.

SBN-13: 978-1477517963
ISBN-10: 1477517960

Also available by Marcus Blakeston

Meadowside
Punk Rock Nursing Home
The Meat Wagon
Bare Knuckle Bitch
Skinhead Away
Biker Sluts versus Flying Saucers

This book is respectfully dedicated to the memory of Richard (Sooty) Sutton, who didn't survive the 1980s.

1 Fucked Up and Wasted

Colin Baxter was already buzzing when he walked through the door of The Queen's Head half an hour after opening time – four cans of beer to go with the bag of chips he had for tea had seen to that. The pub smelled of furniture polish and stale tobacco, masking the sweet scent of malt and hops he expected.

An old couple playing dominos near the door looked up at Colin and tutted to each other. The middle-aged woman behind the bar eyed him with a frown. Colin ignored them all. He was used to getting funny looks – everywhere he went people stared at him, like he was an alien or something. You'd think nobody had ever seen a punk before, the way they always stared. Still, it was their problem, not his.

Colin looked around the otherwise empty pub for his mate, Brian Mathews. He found him sitting by an old Wurlitzer jukebox, and raised his hand in greeting. Brian nodded back and glanced at his watch.

"All right, Col?"

"Yeah, not bad."

Brian reached into his leather jacket and took out a pack of cigarettes and a box of matches. He pulled a cigarette out with his teeth and struck a match on the underside of the table. Colin took out his own cigarettes and leaned over the table to get a light from Brian.

"What did you want to meet in here for?" Colin asked, blowing smoke across the table. "The place is fucking dead."

The old couple playing dominos tutted again. One mumbled something, the other laughed. Colin poked out his tongue at them.

"Happy hour, innit?" Brian said. "Might as well get a few in here while it's cheap, then fuck off down to The White Swan once we're bladdered."

"Yeah, I guess. Or we could just get some drinks in here

and take them with us?"

Brian laughed. "Nah, that barmaid's been watching me like a fucking hawk since I came in. You'd have no chance getting out of here with any drinks."

Colin looked at the barmaid and smiled. She frowned back, hands on hips. Colin walked up to the bar and drummed his fingers on it.

"Pint of bitter please, darling."

"How old are you?" the barmaid asked.

"Erm ... Eighteen?" Colin looked away and tapped his cigarette on the edge of a spotlessly clean ashtray.

The barmaid sighed. Colin looked up in time to see her shake her head and frown. She reached under the bar for a pint glass and filled it from a hand-pump, then put it down on the bar before him.

"Sixty pence," she said.

Colin pulled a crumpled pound note from the pocket of his leather jacket and dropped it into the barmaid's outstretched hand. She sighed again and straightened it out, then held it between her thumb and forefinger as if it was something disgusting while she took it to the till. She returned and dropped Colin's change on the bar.

Colin's eyes strayed to a naked girl on a peanut dispenser behind the bar as he picked up the coins and put them in his pocket. The young blonde woman in the photo had one bag of peanuts hanging over each breast. Colin thought about buying a bag, and wondered if the barmaid would give him a choice between left or right. But something about the way the barmaid stared at him made him change his mind, so he just picked up his pint and walked away.

"I thought you'd have saved that for the gig at the weekend," Colin said, pointing at Brian's Cockney Upstarts T-shirt.

Brian shrugged. "Nah, I'll get me mam to wash it before then. Or wear something else. I haven't decided yet. Besides, everyone else will probably be wearing the same shirt, and I'd rather be an individual than a sheep."

Colin sat down and took a long drink of beer. He sighed and wiped his mouth with the back of his hand.

"Talking of which," Brian said, spinning round in his chair. "What do you reckon to this? Twiglet's brother did it for me, fucking smart or what?"

Colin stared at a white Exploited skull intricately painted onto the back of Brian's leather jacket, with the band's logo beneath it. He nodded.

"Yeah, he's done a good job there. How much?"

Brian turned back and smiled. "Twenty quid."

"Twenty quid? Fucking hell, where did you get that much money from?"

"I haven't paid him yet, I said I'd give him it when me giro comes. Well worth it though, nobody else has got anything like this."

Colin thought about his own leather jacket, the stencilled band names spray-painted onto it, and wished he could afford to have something similar done to his. Not much chance of that though. After he paid his grandmother for board, Colin's giro hardly stretched to a couple of nights out a week and a new record at the weekend. Brian didn't know how lucky he was having working parents who could afford to keep him for free.

The pub door swung open with a loud thud. Colin turned toward it. A young skinhead with an angry scowl on his face swaggered through the door. He was short, just over five feet tall and slightly overweight, and wore a green flight jacket with a Union Jack patch above the left breast. Red braces hung down from a pair of faded denim jeans, the legs of which were turned up six inches to show off a pair of highly polished cherry red fourteen-hole Doc Marten boots.

"Aye up, it's the Munchkin Gestapo," Brian whispered.

Colin laughed. The skinhead glared at him as he walked up to the bar. Still smiling, Colin shook his head and picked up his beer. He gulped it down.

"Sieg Low, Sieg Low, Sieg Low," Brian said, holding a finger under his nose.

Colin spluttered beer across the table. Brian wiped splashes from his face with a frown.

"You dirty bastard," Brian said. "You dirty fucker."

"What a fucking rotter," Colin said, recognising the famous quote from a write-up about it in Melody Maker. He sensed someone standing behind him and turned. The skinhead glared down at him. Colin nodded. "All right, mate. You joining us?"

The skinhead stared at Colin for a few seconds, then shook his head and turned away. He took up a seat a few tables away and sat with his arms folded, staring at his pint glass. Colin shrugged and turned back to his beer. He drained the glass and took it to the bar for a re-fill.

"What's his fucking problem?" Brian asked, nodding at the skinhead when Colin returned.

"Dunno," Colin said with a shrug. "I need a piss anyway. Watch me beer for me." He put the full glass down on the table and headed for the toilet. "All right mate," he said when he passed the skinhead. The skinhead didn't look up.

Inside the toilet, Colin rushed to the communal urinal and pulled down his zip. The toilet door opened and closed behind him. Boots slapped across the tiled floor. Colin took a drag on his cigarette and sighed clouds of smoke while he urinated.

Someone grabbed the spikes on the back of Colin's head and yanked it back. He cried out and dropped his cigarette into the urinal as his forehead crashed into the wall with a dull thud. Blinding white light filled his vision. Before he could do anything his head was wrenched back and slammed into the wall once more. Then a hand grabbed his shoulder and spun him around. He stared at the fuzzy blob before him and shook his head to try and bring it into focus. His eyes widened. The skinhead scowled and raised a fist.

"You fucking cunt," the skinhead yelled, and smacked Colin in the mouth.

Colin's lip stung. He tasted warm copper, felt something dripping down his chin. He raised a hand to his mouth. Rough hands pushed him back against the urinal wall.

"What the fuck are– " Colin began.

The skinhead punched him in the stomach. Colin doubled over, the wind sucked out of him. His legs buckled from beneath him and he slid down the urinal with a faint squeak of leather against aluminium. He looked up at the skinhead as he sat there, piss soaking through his tartan trousers.

"Not so fucking big now, are you cunt?" the skinhead yelled. He shook with rage. His fists clenched and unclenched by his sides.

Colin held his stomach and moaned. He leaned to one side and spat out a glob of blood. "What the fuck?" he asked.

"Like you don't fucking know, you gobby cunt."

Colin shook his head. "Mate, I were just being friendly. You're a fucking psycho."

"Fucking cunt," the skinhead roared, and kicked Colin in the side of the head.

Colin didn't feel the impact, everything just faded to black. The words echoed around his head, "–unt –unt – unt", along with the beginnings of a cackle of laughter. The sounds mingled together before fading to nothing along with his vision.

* * *

Colin opened his eyes and groaned. His head throbbed, his stomach and mouth hurt, and he was soaking wet. He lay in the urinal a few seconds while he figured out where he was, then sat up and looked around. Bubbly, foul-smelling liquid dripped down his face. He wiped it away and felt a sharp stabbing pain in his forehead when his hand brushed against it. He explored the area with his fingertips and winced when he touched a tender, round lump.

The toilet door opened. Colin startled, fearing it might be the skinhead returning to finish him off. But as the figure loomed closer, Colin relaxed. It was just one of the domino players from the bar.

The old man leaned over him and smiled. "The sit down bogs is over there, lad," he said, pointing at a cubicle door. He laughed raspingly, then stepped up to the urinal a few feet from where Colin sat.

Colin leaned forward onto his hands and knees and crawled out of the urinal just as a fresh torrent of urine made its way toward him. He stumbled to his feet and spat a glob of blood onto the tiled floor. He realised he still had his penis out, and pushed it back in and zipped up.

The old man looked over his shoulder and smiled. "Is that the new fashion then?" he asked.

Colin staggered to the sink to look at his battered face in the mirror. His bottom lip was split and oozing blood. There was a red lump the size of a golf ball on the left side of his forehead, and the beginnings of a bruise just above his right ear. The spikes he had spent so long twisting his hair into were all wilted and bent out of shape, frothy with soap bubbles. A wave of nausea hit him. He leaned over the sink and retched. Blood, beer and half-digested chips splattered into the porcelain bowl.

"Can't take your beer, that's your trouble," the old man said, walking past. "You should stick to shandy, lad."

Colin turned on the cold water tap and splashed water onto his face, then ran his hands through his hair. He tried to mould it back into shape but it was too wet for that. He reached for a paper towel but the dispenser was empty. He sighed, took a final look at his reflection in the mirror, and walked back into the bar.

Brian's eyes widened. "Fucking hell, what's happened to you?" he asked.

Colin attempted a smile as he staggered back to his seat, and winced at a sharp pain in his lip. "That fucking skinhead cunt smacked me in the bogs." He looked around the deserted pub. The old couple with the dominos pointed and laughed at him. "Where is the bastard?"

"Went ages ago. You all right then? You look a right fucking mess."

"Yeah well, I've been better."

"Mate, if I'd known I would've come in and helped you out. So what happened then?"

"Took me by surprise, didn't he? Fucking little coward whacked me while I were having a piss."

"Fucking hell, what a cunt," Brian said, shaking his head. He lit a cigarette and took a deep drag, exhaling the smoke in Colin's direction. "You want me to take you home or something?"

Colin shrugged and reached for his beer. "Nah, I'll be all right." His hand shook as he raised the glass to take a sip. Searing pain shot through his mouth. Colin jerked the glass away, spilling beer down his already wet clothes.

Brian looked at Colin and raised an eyebrow. He smirked. "You'll need to drink it with a straw, mate. I can remember when me brother gave me a fat lip years ago, it fucking killed for ages."

Colin put the glass down and reached into his leather jacket pocket for his cigarettes. The gold pack was damp, and his fingers sank in as he gripped it. He flipped up the lid, took hold of a cigarette, raised it to his mouth–

–and looked down at the soggy brown filter tip in his hand, the rest of the cigarette still in the packet.

"Oh for fuck's sake!" Colin flicked the cigarette filter

away and turned to Brian. "Give us a fag Bri, mine are all wet."

Brian tossed his cigarette pack across the table and held out his own cigarette for Colin to light one from. Colin closed his eyes and sighed as he exhaled. The nicotine rush cleared his head a little. He opened his eyes and looked at his beer longingly, wishing he could drink it without pain. He decided Brian's idea of using a straw wasn't as daft as it sounded, and looked toward the bar. The barmaid stared at him, her arms folded. She frowned. Colin placed his hands on the table and pushed himself to his feet. The table wobbled under his weight, and Brian grabbed his pint glass to stop it from toppling over.

"Have you got any straws?" Colin asked the barmaid.

She shook her head, frowning. "I'm not serving you looking like that. You'll have to leave."

"What?" Colin said. "I haven't done nothing. I got attacked in the bogs."

"I don't care, this is a respectable pub. People come here for a quiet drink, they don't want to look at louts like you and your friend over there. Now get out, you're barred."

Colin knocked over an empty stool and glared at her. "It's a fucking shit pub anyway." He looked at Brian, who frowned back at him.

Outside, Colin shivered in the cold while he waited for Brian to finish urinating against a wall. A dark blue car pulled up at the kerb just as Brian finished, and its tinted passenger-side window rolled down. A young man wearing a suit and tie leaned out, then beckoned Brian over with his fingers. Brian walked up to the car and leaned down to look inside.

"What's up, mate?" he asked.

"SID'S DEAD!" the man shouted.

The driver of the car, another young man in a suit and tie, laughed and aimed a bottle of tomato sauce over the passenger's shoulder. He squeezed the soft plastic bottle and a stream of red tomato sauce flew at Brian. Brian jumped back, but couldn't avoid his face and clothes being splattered with it.

"You fucking cunt," Brian shouted. He reached for the car's door handle and pulled, but the door was locked. He reached through the open window and grabbed a handful of the passenger's shirt. The car sped away with a squeal of tyres, causing Brian to withdraw his hand quickly.

"FUCKING TOSSERS!" Brian shouted after the car as it raced to the end of the street. It disappeared around the corner with another squeal of tyres. Brian turned to Colin. "Did you see that?"

Colin nodded. "Yeah. Fucking trendy wankers, they're worse than fucking skinheads."

Brian took a handkerchief from his jeans pocket and wiped tomato sauce from his face, then dabbed at the smears on his leather jacket and T-shirt. "As if anyone cares about that drugged up cunt anyway. He couldn't even fucking play."

"Yeah," Colin said, not really interested. He had heard Brian's tirade on the relative merits of Sid Vicious and Ronnie Biggs versus Glen Matlock and Johnny Rotten many times before and had no desire to hear it again. "We going to The White Swan then, before I sober up too much?"

Without waiting for an answer, Colin marched unsteadily up the street.

* * *

Trog punched the door of The Black Bull, wishing it could be the gobby punk's head. It was bad enough having his bird yelling and screaming at him for no reason, then stamping off in a sulk. But having someone call him a 'fucking rotter' just tipped him over the edge. Probably some sort of layabout student. Well that's one student who won't be giving him any lip next time.

Trog would have done his mate too if he had the chance. He'd waited for them outside the Queen's Head, but neither of the useless pricks had come out. If someone from The Black Bull had been smacked like that the whole fucking pub would be out there looking for revenge. Because that's what skins do. They look after their own.

The rowdy sounds of a Cockney Upstarts song playing on the jukebox blasted out when Trog pushed open the door and entered the smoke-filled lounge. He waved at a group of skinheads taking up the far corner and nodded at the old codger nursing a half by the door. Alf, his name was, but everyone called him 'H', short for Half Pint Alf because that half sitting before him would last all night. He was the last of the old time Black Bull regulars, from before the town's skinheads moved in and turned it into their own regular hang-out. The stubborn old bastard just plain refused to move on, and had become part of the furniture.

"Lager, Trog?"

Trog leaned on the bar and nodded. "Yeah, cheers Mandy."

Mandy pulled Trog a pint of lager and placed it on a bar towel before him. She smiled as she held out her hand. "Cheer up Trog, might never happen."

Trog shrugged, staring at his pint. "It already has."

"Oh?"

Trog reached into his flight jacket and pulled out a leather wallet. He peeled off a five pound note and handed it to Mandy. "Don't worry about it, just a rough day that's all. Here, get yourself a drink on me."

Mandy poured herself a pint of lager and blackcurrant, handed Trog his change, and leaned her elbows on the bar. She cradled her face and smiled at him. "You want to tell me about it?"

"Nah, not really. Just a bust up with me bird, she'll get over it."

Mandy winked. "Well if she doesn't, it's her loss."

Trog laughed and nodded. "Yeah, too fucking right."

Trog knew Mandy was an ex-skinbyrd from the 1970s, an original. That was probably why she didn't mind the skinheads moving into The Black Bull, even after they chased out all the regulars. They didn't know this at the time; she was just a normal-looking older bird by then, the skinhead look being long gone. But Mandy always had a friendly smile for the young skinheads, and the more they got to know her the more she revealed of her own youth. The Shefferham gang she ran with, the fights she got into on the terraces, her tussles with bikers and the law. Everyone was enthralled with her. Even more so when she re-donned a feather-cut hairstyle and said she'd had enough of living in disguise. Trog had a lot of respect for that. Most women her age had settled down into a life of mediocrity long ago.

"I think she might have dumped me for good this time though," Trog said. He took a sip of lager and eyed Mandy over the rim.

"Oh yeah?"

"Yeah. We were on our way to the cinema to watch Death Wish II when she kicked off. I waved to this bird I knew from school and Barbara had a fucking fit about it. Said I were screwing her behind her back."

"And are you?" Mandy asked, the faint trace of a smile on her face.

"No, am I fuck. I don't screw around like that, it's not right is it? Like I said, it were just some bird I knew from school. Trendy bird as well. And she were with some bloke, some fucking yeti, so she obviously likes them hairy. But Barbara weren't having none of it, she said it were obvious I'd been fucking this bird from the way she looked at me."

"So what did you say?"

"I didn't get the chance to say anything. She got all fucking hysterical right there in the street, and then lunged at me and tried to scratch me face. So I gave her a slap, just to calm her down like. Then she just stamped off, calling me all sorts, so I went into the nearest boozer for a drink just to calm meself down a bit."

Mandy shook her head, still smiling. "Didn't work though, did it?"

"Yeah well, it probably would've worked if it weren't for some fucking student giving it the big gob. That just wound me up even more. Called me a fucking rotter, would you believe?" Mandy laughed. "Anyway, I think it's definitely over with Barbara this time. It's not really been right between us for quite a while now; I think she were just looking for an excuse, really."

"Never mind, plenty more fish, eh?"

Trog looked into Mandy's deep blue eyes and held her stare. He smiled and picked up his lager, then turned to leave. "Yeah, I guess. Anyway, I'll see you later."

"Trog, you fat bastard," one of the skinheads yelled as he approached.

Trog grinned. "Aye up Stew, you skinny cunt, how's it hanging?"

Stew, a cigarette in his mouth, hooked his thumbs under his braces and stretched them out. "Hanging well, Trog. How's it with yours?"

"Yeah, not bad." Trog squeezed himself between Stew and an older skinhead, Don, and sat down on a long padded bench.

"Oi Trog, you going down to Shefferham for the Cockney Upstarts gig on Saturday then?" Don asked.

"Too fucking right I am," Trog said. "Wouldn't miss it for the fucking world."

* * *

Trog slammed an empty pint glass down on the table. "You up for another drink then, Don?"

Don shook his head. "Nah mate, I'm skint. Giro doesn't

come until next week."

"No worries, I'll get you one. You can pay me back at the Cockney Upstarts gig. Anyone else want one?" Trog added, looking at the other faces sitting around the table. He was inundated with requests for drinks, and pulled out his wallet. "Here's a tenner, get a pint for everyone. I got a good bonus this week, might as well share the wealth."

Don took the ten pound note and rose to his feet. "Cheers Trog, you're a star."

"No worries, mate. Money's for spending, innit? Get one for Mandy as well."

Don smiled. "You want me to give Mandy one? No fucking problem, mate."

Trog watched Don swagger to the bar and place his order. Mandy laughed and looked in Trog's direction. He raised a hand and smiled back. Don returned with the drinks on a round metal tray and placed it down in the centre of the table. Trog scooped up his change from the edge of the tray and put it in his flight jacket pocket.

"I told Mandy you said to give her one from you," Don said, "but she said she'd rather you give her one yourself. I reckon you're in there, mate."

Trog laughed. "Yeah, right. Chance would be a fine thing."

"No, straight up. But if you're not interested I don't mind slipping her a length for you."

Trog looked across at Mandy. She smiled and waved, then opened the bar flap.

"Aye up," Don said, "she's coming over. I hope you've got your clean undies on."

"Piss off," Trog said, smiling, "you're just fucking jealous."

"Who fucking wouldn't be, fit old bird like that?"

Mandy walked up to the jukebox and put a coin in the slot, then pressed buttons on the front. An old ska record started playing and Mandy's arms and hips swayed to it as she mouthed the words to the song.

"Go on then Trog," Ian said, grinning. He winked at Don. "Now's your chance, mate. Get in there and show her some of your fancy footwork."

Trog took a gulp of lager and shook his head. "What, and have you cunts take the piss? Anyway I don't like that fucking ska stuff, never have."

"Yeah, it's a right fucking horrible noise," Don said with a scowl. "What's she doing dancing to that fucking shite?"

"Shows what you know," Ian said. "It's better than that fucking Oi bollocks you listen to. Can't even fucking play, most of them."

"What, and these can? They all sound the same these fucking bongo bands."

"Fuck off bongo bands. This is proper skinhead music, this is. And they're not fucking bongos anyway. Sounds nothing like bongos."

"Is it fuck proper skinhead music. They're not even fucking white, never mind skinheads. Bunch of fucking wogs, half of them."

"I don't like it either," Stew said, "but they didn't have no Skrewdriver in the olden days, so it stands to reason old birds like Mandy over there would be into it."

"Great, another fucking commie," Don said, shaking his head.

"Fuck off, I ain't no fucking commie. I'm just saying it were different in the old days, that's all."

"Oh, give it a fucking rest," Trog said. "Who gives a fuck about any of that bollocks?"

"Yeah well," Don said, reaching into his flight jacket for a pack of cigarettes, "I'm only saying skinhead bands should be white or there's no fucking point to them."

"Crash the ash then, Adolf," Ian said. Don took out a cigarette and tossed the pack across the table. Ian smiled as he picked it up. "Redistribution of wealth in action. So who's the fucking commie now then?"

Trog sighed and shook his head. He turned back to watch Mandy dance.

* * *

The White Swan was packed with trendies, standing room only. An old Slade song played on the jukebox, and somewhere behind the crush around the bar a group of youths shouted along tunelessly with it. Colin would know those voices anywhere. He nodded to Brian.

"The gang's all here."

A young couple stood before the jukebox, arguing about what songs they should spend their money on. The girl, in a pink and yellow spotted summer dress, wanted Adam and the Ants. The boy, sporting a denim jacket, wanted Thin Lizzy.

"Scuse us, darling," Brian said, and barged past the couple.

"Hey, watch it, you—" the girl began, then took in the Exploited skull painted on the back of Brian's leather jacket. She turned to her boyfriend and frowned. "Bloody yobs," she said when Brian was out of earshot.

"Fucking trendies," Colin said, glaring at her.

The girl gaped at Colin and sniffed. She wrinkled her nose and stepped back, closer to the jukebox. "Did you see that?" Colin heard her say as he walked away.

Brian was talking to Twiglet, a gangly half-caste youth with blotches of darker-coloured skin covering his face, when Colin reached the far side of the pub. He was telling him about what had happened in The Queen's Head. Twiglet's massive afro hairstyle bobbed as he nodded his head in sympathy. Mike Thornton, in faded denim jeans and a plain black sweatshirt, looked on, frowning. Stiggy swayed by Brian's side, holding a pint of cider. Even from a distance Colin could smell the solvents wafting off him.

"Colin, you cunt," Mike shouted when he saw Colin. "I hear you got twatted by a midget. Fucking show up or what?"

Colin gave him a scowl and a quick V-sign before slinking into the gents to see if he could rescue what was left of his hair spikes. When he returned he expected more snide comments, but everyone seemed genuinely concerned about what had happened to him.

"Fucking skinheads," Stiggy said. "We should do one of *them*, see how they fucking like it."

"Yeah," Mike agreed, nodding. He took a gulp of his beer.

"There was a bunch of skinheads at the back of the bus the other day making fucking monkey noises at me," Twiglet said.

Mike shook his head. "Mate, that's fucking bang out of order. What did you do?"

"Well what do you think I did? I'm not fucking daft, I just ignored them and made a run for it as soon as I got off."

Mike nodded. "Yeah, you probably did right, mate. We should still do something about it though. Can't let the bastards get away with something like that."

Twiglet shook his head. "Nah, not really worth it. Anyway, skinheads all look the same to me. We'd only end up battering the wrong ones."

"Would that matter?" Mike said with a sly grin. He drained the last of his beer and set off for the bar. Brian followed him.

"Oi Bri," Colin shouted, "get me one while you're there, I'll give you the money when you get back." Brian turned and gave him a thumbs up. "And get me a straw as well."

"What do you reckon then, Col," Stiggy said, "find a skinhead and do the cunt, or what?"

Colin was about to tell Stiggy he'd rather leave it when

the opening bars of a Bruce Springsteen song, Born To Run, drowned him out. Mike cheered its arrival from the bar.

"Not this fucking shite again," Twiglet said, covering his ears.

Colin groaned, it was the worst song he'd ever heard and seemed to be playing on the jukebox in The White Swan every ten minutes or so. He was just as sick of hearing it as Twiglet. He could hear Mike shouting along to it from the bar, and wished he would shut up. He didn't understand what Mike saw in that type of music. Mike wasn't a punk, he was just someone Twiglet was at school with, but he did like Sham 69 and Cockney Upstarts. As well as Slade, Garry Glitter, and boring old fart music like Bruce fucking Springsteen – there was just no logic in it.

When the song reached its chorus, Twiglet made up his own words and shouted them over the music.

"Scum like us, maybe we don't give a fu-uck!"

Colin smiled and joined in at the next chorus. A group of trendies at a nearby table glared at them, then stood up to leave. Colin, Stiggy and Twiglet pushed past them to claim the table before anyone else had the same idea. They made space for Mike when he arrived.

Brian returned with two pints of bitter and put one down in front of Colin with a pink, curly plastic straw floating in it. Shaped like a helter-skelter, it had a love-heart shaped handle near the top with the words *I love Babycham* printed on it.

"What the fuck's this?" Colin asked with a scowl.

"It's all they had mate," Brian said, grinning.

Colin put the straw to the corner of his mouth and sucked. The beer slowly twirled its way up the straw and into his mouth. Mike and Twiglet both laughed as they watched.

"Fuck off, you're only jealous," Colin said. He cradled his beer in one hand and toyed with the straw with the other, twirling it between his thumb and forefinger.

"You and Brian going down to Shefferham on Saturday for the Cockney Upstarts gig?" Twiglet asked.

Colin looked up and nodded. "Yeah, of course. Can't miss something like that, can we? It's not like they come this far north often, and it'd cost a fucking bomb to see them in that London of theirs."

Stiggy scowled. "Fucking skinhead band aren't they?"

"Are they fuck," Brian said. "They were a punk band years before all them baldy cunts latched onto them. Anyway, I heard Manny doesn't like skinheads either. One time at this open air gig he picked up this fucking metal spike and chased loads of skinheads across a field with it. That's what I heard, anyway."

"That would have been funny to watch," Stiggy said. "I heard he throws a pig's head into the audience at the end of their show as well. It'd be fucking brilliant if he twatted some skinhead in the face with it."

"Where'd you hear that bollocks?" Twiglet asked.

"No, it's true," Stiggy said, "it were in me dad's paper ages ago."

"What paper were that then?"

"Dunno, the one me dad gets. There was a photo of it and everything."

"It must be fucking true then, if it were in your dad's paper," Brian said, smiling and shaking his head. "Funny they never mentioned it in Sounds or the NME."

"Well we'll find out on Saturday then, won't we?" Stiggy said. "I bet you a quid he does."

"You're fucking on," Brian said. "Easiest money I'll ever make." He looked at Twiglet. "So who else is going then?"

"Spazzo's deffo going," Twiglet said. "Not sure about anyone else yet. There's a few more that said they might go if they can scrounge enough money together. We're meeting up at the train station buffet at six, probably see you there."

"Six?" Colin said. "I'll be at home having me tea then. What time's the train?"

"Half past. But the next one's not until eight so if you miss it we won't be waiting for you."

"Fuck your tea," Brian said. "We'll get some chips or something when we get to Shefferham."

* * *

When the bell rang for last orders, Colin still had over half a pint left. Drinking through a straw, he just couldn't compete with the others, and they were already two pints ahead of him. He knew there was no point going to the bar himself, he had already tried that and the barman had refused to serve him. So he gave Brian two pound notes and told him to get a can of beer to go and a pack of cigarettes. Mike, Stiggy and Twiglet then decided they didn't see the point all of them joining the scrum around the bar, so they too gave Brian their orders.

Brian returned a few minutes later with the drinks cradled precariously in his hands and plonked them down on the table. He reached into his leather jacket and pulled out a can of Colt 45, then rolled it across the table to Colin. Colin placed his hand on top of the can to stop it rolling onto the floor.

"Where's me fags?" Colin asked. He picked up the beer can and studied it. "Fucking lager?"

Brian tossed him a pack of cigarettes and shrugged. "They didn't have no bitter in cans," he said. "Anyway, the bloke behind the bar said it were strong stuff, and that's what counts, right? If you don't want it, I'll have it."

"I never said I didn't want it. Just that it's fucking lager." Colin put the can down and opened the cigarette pack. He took one out and lit it.

"No fucking way," Mike said, staring at the beer can.

"What?" Twiglet asked.

Mike pointed. "There's a picture of a deformed punk

with a massive cock on the side of it."

"Yeah, right." Twiglet leaned across the table and peered at the can. "Fucking hell, it has too! It must be beer for fucking nob-heads."

"Or birds that like deformed punks," Mike said, grinning. "There's hope for you yet, Col. As long as you've got a massive cock like that, anyway."

"It's a fucking stonker, but it's not as big as mine," Twiglet said.

"What, you've compared cocks with Mr Pink Straw over there? You dirty fucker."

"What? No, fuck off. I mean the one on the can's a fucking stonker."

Colin picked up the can and spun it around in his hand but couldn't focus his eyes on it well enough to make out any detail. "Where's this cock then?"

"There!" Twiglet pointed at a small red blob printed on the side of the can. Colin squinted at it and put a hand over one eye, but he still couldn't bring it into focus.

"Let's have a look then," Brian said, snatching the can from Colin's hand.

"Oi, get off you cunt." Colin made a grab for the can, but Brian was too quick for him. He spun around on his stool and turned his back on Colin.

"It's a fucking horse, you daft bastards."

Mike stood up and bent over to look at the can in Brian's hand. "Is it fuck. It looks nothing like a fucking horse. What's that sticking out of its head then?" He tapped the top of the picture with his finger.

"That's not its head, that's its arse. And it's a leg that's sticking out of it."

"What, and it's got a mohican growing out of its arse?"

"That's its tail. It's a fucking horse."

"Is it fuck, it's a bloke." Mike pointed at the picture to emphasise his points. "Look, there's two eyes and a nose under the mohican. And some pubes between his legs, look ... and if it were a horse its cock would be at the other end, up there."

Brian gave the can a quick shake before handing it back to Colin. "It's still a fucking horse. That's why it's called Colt 45. Colt is another name for a horse."

"Nah, a Colt 45 is a gun. Like a pistol. And a Sex Pistol is a cock as well, so it must be a punk with a big cock. Stands to reason, doesn't it?"

Brian shook his head and sighed. "Yeah, whatever."

"Crack it then, Col," Twiglet said. "I want to see what this Cock 45 stuff tastes like."

"Nah, I'm saving it for the bus. I've still got this to drink, yet."

"Best hurry up then," Brian said, picking up his beer. "Last bus goes in about twenty minutes."

* * *

Mandy rang the bell hanging over the bar of The Black Bull for the third time. Nobody took any notice. She walked over to the jukebox and switched it off at the mains, silencing the new Blitz single mid-song. Don groaned and told her to put it back on again.

"Can you drink up now, please?" Mandy shouted. She returned to the bar and rang the bell again. "Hello? It's time to go home."

"All right Mandy, keep your knickers on," Ian said. "We've not finished our beer yet."

"Well hurry up then. I want to go home even if you don't." Mandy walked over to the skinheads and stood before them, hands on hips.

"Can't we have a lock-in?" Don asked.

Mandy shook her head. "Not tonight, I've got other plans." She looked at Trog and caught his eye. "Trog, can you give me a hand to close up?"

Trog drained the last of his lager and nodded. "Yeah, no

worries, Mandy." He put the empty glass down and rose to his feet. "Right, you cunts. You heard Mandy. It's time to get fucked off home."

A few grumbled about the lack of a proper ten minute drinking up time, but they all soon finished off their drinks and shuffled toward the door. Trog helped Mandy collect the empty glasses and put them down on the bar.

"Night then, Mandy," he said, and turned to leave. Don was waiting for him by the door. The others were outside, larking about and taking the piss out of passing trendies.

"Wait a minute, Trog," Mandy called out. "Give us a minute to lock up and you can walk me home if you like?"

Trog turned and looked at her. She smiled and winked.

"Get in there, you jammy fucking bastard," Don said, nudging Trog in the ribs.

Trog grinned. "I'll see you cunts on Saturday then."

"Give her one for me," Don said as he left. Mandy closed the door behind him and bolted it.

"I thought you wanted me to walk you home?" Trog asked.

Mandy smiled and ran her finger tips down Trog's braces, then took one in each hand and pulled him closer. "You can do that later," she said.

2 Bored Teenagers

Colin felt something wet slithering across his face. He groaned and turned away, pulled the bedcovers over his head. Something pounced on him, dug at the covers and pulled them down. The wet thing was back, leaving trails of slime on Colin's cheek.

Colin's eyes fluttered open. Bright sunlight streamed through a gap between the bedroom curtains and made him squint. His head throbbed, and his mouth felt like someone had fitted a shag-pile carpet in there while he slept. The dog licked him again.

"Fucking hell Prince, get off me," he groaned, and pushed the brown mongrel dog off the bed. He rolled over to go back to sleep. The dog jumped back onto the bed and licked him again.

"Fuck off, you mutt!"

Colin pushed the dog's head away from his face. The dog grabbed Colin's pyjama shirt sleeve and shook it, growling. Colin pulled back. The dog squatted down on its hind legs to tug harder.

"All right, fucking hell. I'll get up."

Colin threw back the covers and sat up, then looked at a clock on the bedside table. It wasn't even ten o'clock yet, far too early to be awake. Colin groaned and stood up. The dog bounded around his feet, jumping up to lick his face. Colin sidestepped the dog and darted into the bathroom for a piss.

"That you Colin?"

Colin heard the faint voice from the living room over the sound of a blaring TV set as he descended the stairs. The dog followed close behind.

"No, it's a burglar," Colin shouted back.

"Make us a cup of tea and a sarnie then."

"Okay, Gran."

Colin went into the kitchen and made two bread and dripping sandwiches and two mugs of tea. He put one sandwich on a plate and stuffed half the other one into his mouth and ate it while he waited for the tea to brew. He finished off the rest, then carried the plate and two mugs into the living room.

Colin put the plate down on the arm of his grandmother's chair, then balanced a mug next to it. He took the other mug and sat down on the settee with a sigh. The dog bounded up next to him.

"So what time did you roll in last night then?" his grandmother asked, without looking away from the television. A coloured man wearing spandex leapt around on the screen, encouraging viewers to join him for their morning exercise.

"Don't know," Colin said. "Probably late."

He could dimly remember being sick on the bus, and both he and Brian being thrown off by the irate bus driver, but the long walk home was still a blur. He had a distant recollection of climbing over the park fence and lying on his back on the roundabout while Brian spun him around, but wasn't sure if that was a dream or not. It seemed a daft thing to do when the world would already be spinning out of control due to excess alcohol, but it probably made sense at the time.

"What's happened to your face?"

Colin looked up, saw his grandmother peering at him. He shrugged and looked away. "Been dancing," he mumbled. "Caught a few elbows in the face."

She grunted, then laughed and shook her head. "I don't know, you punk rockers you're all as daft as brushes." She picked up her sandwich and bit into it. "Of course, we had proper dancing in my day," she said.

"Yes Gran," Colin said, and tuned out while his grandmother related one of her stories about her youthful exploits. He had already heard them all countless times. How you could buy just about anything you wanted with an empty jam jar or pop bottle, how nice and polite everyone was in the old days, and how much better everything used to be.

Colin had lived with his grandmother for as long as he could remember. His father left soon after he was born, saying he couldn't handle the responsibility of another mouth to feed. His mother left a year later, when one of her boyfriends gave her an ultimatum – him or the kid. She chose the boyfriend, so Colin was dumped on his grandmother and he never saw her again. Colin was too young to know anything about all this, of course, and didn't remember either of his parents, but this was what his grandmother told him had happened, and he had no reason to doubt her.

Colin drank his tea and pushed the dog from his lap. "I'm going back to bed," he said.

His grandmother looked up sharply. "What? You've only just got up."

"Yeah, I don't feel too good. Must've had a bad pint or something. I'm gonna go and lie down for a bit."

Upstairs, Colin shut the bedroom door before the dog had a chance to dart through it. The dog whined and scratched at the door for a few minutes, then gave up. Colin spread his wet cigarettes out along the windowsill and got back into bed. He closed his eyes and relived the events of the previous night. He didn't understand why the skinhead had attacked him. If it had been a trendy it would make sense, trendies were always keen on punk bashing. But a skinhead? They weren't vastly different from punks themselves, they even liked the same type of music. It just didn't make sense.

* * *

"I'm off out now Gran, see you later," Colin shouted from the hallway. He picked up his leather jacket from the banister and shuffled into it. The sleeves were still a bit damp from the previous night, but nothing he couldn't put up with.

It was half-past one, a much more civilised time to be up and about. Colin's hangover was almost gone, thanks to a fry-up and several more mugs of tea, and he was sure he'd be able to shrug the rest of it off once he got outside. His hair was standing proud and erect once again, and he wore a fresh set of clothes. It was an Exploited and tiger-print trousers day, he felt it as soon as he woke up for the second time that day.

"Bye Colin," his grandmother called out from the living room. "Don't forget it's your Granddad's birthday tomorrow, you said you would take me to see him."

Colin had forgotten, but he didn't let on. "I will," he shouted, and closed the door behind him.

To Colin, Granddad was just an old black and white photograph on the living room sideboard. A photograph Colin was never allowed to touch without being yelled at to leave it alone. His grandfather died less than a year after he came home from the war, just before Colin's mother was born. He was trapped in a cave-in down the local coal mine, and it took his co-workers three days to dig him out. By then he had suffocated to death.

Colin knew he had died a long time ago, but didn't find out the circumstances of his death until the day his grandmother caught him filling in an application form for the National Coal Board, soon after he left school. "You're not working there," his grandmother said when she saw the form, and tore it up in front of him.

Colin caught a bus into town and headed into the shopping centre. He found Brian sitting on a bench outside Woolworths, reading Sounds.

"About fucking time," Brian said, looking up from the newspaper. "Have a good lie in, did you?"

Colin shrugged, then sat down next to him. "Felt a bit rough so I went back to bed. Why, how long you been here?"

"Fucking ages. I went to sign on this morning, didn't I?"

"Anything interesting this week?" Colin asked, nodding at Brian's newspaper.

Brian turned back a few pages and held it up. "There's a Beki Bondage interview, it says they've got a new album coming out soon."

"Yeah? I'll have to start saving up then. What's Pressbutton up to this week?"

"Dunno, I haven't got that far yet. I was reading the gig reviews, there's one for Cockney Upstarts in Camden."

"It say anything about pigs' heads?"

Brian laughed. "Nah, does it fuck." He closed the newspaper, then folded it up and balanced it on his knee while he took out his cigarettes.

Colin reached out for the newspaper and turned to the back pages to read the cartoons. He laughed. "Fucking hell, it gets madder. There's a woman with light bulbs for tits. I don't know what that Curt Vile is on, but I wouldn't mind having some." He folded the newspaper up with the comic strip on top and handed it back to Brian.

"Nah, drugs are for fucking hippies," Brian said. He smiled and shook his head while he read the comic strip. After he finished he rolled the paper up and stuffed it into the inside pocket of his leather jacket.

A three-year-old girl skipped past, then turned and stared at Colin and Brian. She pointed excitedly. "Look, mummy! Mummy, look! Look at the funny men!"

Colin pulled a face at the child, then raised his arms and roared. She stepped back and squealed in delight. A woman grabbed the girl's arm and shook her. "That's naughty," she said, "don't point at strange men." The girl looked back over her shoulder as she was pulled away. Colin poked out his tongue at her.

"So what are we doing today then?" Colin asked.

Brian shrugged. "Dunno. Just hang out here, I guess. Not much else to do."

* * *

Later, Colin and Brian were in a record shop on the first floor, looking in the bargain bin for anything interesting among the ex-chart singles. Two punk girls flicked through albums on a rack nearby. One kept looking over her shoulder, but every time Colin caught her eye she looked away.

"Nothing here worth having," Brian said.

"Speak for yourself," Colin said. He nodded at the two girls.

Brian looked and smiled, then walked up to them. "All right?"

The girls looked around and nodded to Brian, then looked at each other and smirked. One pulled out a punk compilation album and flipped it over. Colin walked over and peered over her shoulder at the band names printed on it.

"Looks pretty good," he said. "You buying it then?"

"Nah," the girl said. "Can't afford it." She put the album back in the rack and turned to Colin. "So what happened to your face then?"

Colin felt his cheeks burn, and subconsciously touched the still-tender lump on his forehead. He thought about telling her the truth, then changed his mind. She'd probably think he was a wuss.

"Got it while I were dancing."

Brian snorted, but didn't contradict him. The girl's eyes widened. "What, you got all that from dancing?"

Brian nodded. "Yeah, he's quite the dancer. You should see him in action some time."

"Nah, you're all right." She turned to leave. "Come on, Becky."

"Beki?" Colin asked. "What, like as in Beki Bondage?"

Becky smiled. "No, as in Rebecca."

"What's your mate's name then, Becky?" Brian asked.

"Kaz."

"Bye then, Kaz," Brian said, waving. "See you, Becky." As they left he shouted after them. "I'm Brian. The ugly guy is called Colin."

"Fuck you," Colin said, grinning. He turned to the album rack and flicked through them while Brian went to have a look at new single releases.

When they left the record shop Becky and Kaz were leaning over the balcony outside, pointing and laughing at shoppers below. Brian sang the opening lines to Last Rockers as he and Colin walked past them. Becky looked around and smiled.

Colin and Brian wandered around the upper level of the shopping centre without any specific destination in mind. Brian paused outside a hifi shop and looked through the window. Colin knew neither of them could afford any of the prices being asked, but that didn't stop Brian pointing out which ones he was planning to buy in the near future. Colin leaned his back against the shop window and sighed. He was about to take out his cigarettes when he saw Becky and Kaz dart into a nearby shop. As he continued watching, Becky peered out from the shop doorway and ducked back out of sight. Colin smiled to himself and turned to look in the hifi shop window.

"I think them birds are following us," he said.

Brian turned and looked. "Yeah?"

"Yeah. Let's go and talk to them."

Brian shook his head. "Nah, I've got a better idea."

Colin and Brian walked on. They kept an eye on reflections in shop windows to make sure they were still being followed, and veered off into Woolworths. They passed aisles of children's clothes, then toys, and rode down the escalator to ground level.

A fat security guard glared at them from the kitchenware area, then ducked down to hide behind some boxes. Colin waved to him, he scowled back. Colin knew they would be carefully watched until they left Woolworths, with the security guard trying to hide his massive bulk behind whatever was to hand every time they turned around. Normally they would have some fun with him, at least until one of the other security guards showed up and they were escorted off the premises, but Brian seemed to have other ideas.

Colin looked up and saw Becky and Kaz duck out of sight at the top of the escalator. He shrugged to himself and followed Brian to the music section near the ground floor exit. Through strategically placed anti-shoplifter mirrors he saw the security guard limping after him.

Brian stood by a life-size cardboard cut-out of Abba advertising a forthcoming greatest hits compilation. "Hurry up, get behind here," he said when Colin approached.

"What for?"

"You'll see."

Colin glanced over his shoulder. The security guard dodged into a shopping aisle and peered out from its edge. Colin joined Brian behind the Abba cut-out and crouched down beside him.

"You know he's already seen us?"

"Who?" Brian asked.

"Fucking Sergeant Hoppalong, he's been following us since we came downstairs."

Brian placed a finger over his mouth and cocked his head to one side. Colin heard Becky and Kaz talking nearby.

"They must have gone out," one said.

"Yeah well, they can't have gone far," the other replied.

Brian nodded to Colin. "Now," he mouthed silently, and leaped out from behind Abba with a roar. The girls jumped and squealed, then spun around to face him. Colin walked out and stood beside Brian.

"You looking for us?" Brian asked.

"As if," Kaz said with a shrug.

"Yeah," Becky said. "We were wondering if you were going to The Juggler's Rest on Friday? There's a band on this week."

"Who's on?" Colin asked.

"The Astronauts?"

"Never heard of them, are they any good?"

Brian elbowed Colin in the ribs. "Does it matter? Yeah, of course we'll be going."

Becky smiled. "Might see you there, then," she said, and they both turned and walked away.

Colin watched them pass the security guard on their way to the exit. The man seemed torn between following the girls or resuming his vigil of Colin and Brian.

"You got any money?" Colin asked.

Brian shrugged. "Not much, why?"

"I'm fucking starving. Let's go back upstairs and get a Criss-Cross and a pot of tea."

* * *

"Fucking hell, look at the state of that cunt."

Colin swivelled in his bucket seat to see what Brian was pointing at. Stiggy lurched between the tables in the Woolworths café, heading in the direction of the toilets. His ripped Discharge T-shirt clung to his chest, his baggy green camouflage trousers were caked in mud. Water dripped from his uncombed mass of hair.

"All right, Stiggy?" Colin called out.

Stiggy looked in their direction, nodded, then veered toward their table. He took up a seat next to Brian, who wrinkled his nose at the strong chemical solvent odour on

Stiggy's breath.

"All right, Col. Giz a drink, I'm fucking freezing." Without waiting for a reply, Stiggy reached out for Colin's tea mug and cupped his hands around it. Colin saw his knuckles were bruised and scuffed. Stiggy lifted the mug to his mouth and breathed into it a few times before he took a drink.

"What happened to your hands?" Colin asked.

Stiggy put the mug down and stretched out his hands, palms down, on the table. He looked puzzled for a few seconds, then grinned and nodded. "Oh yeah, I forgot. Me and Mike found a skinhead on the way home last night and did the cunt. Battered him fucking senseless. You should've heard him beg, it were funny as fuck."

"I wish I'd been there to see it," Colin said. "What did he look like?"

"Like a fucking mess after we'd finished with him."

"No, I mean before. Was he short?" Colin held out a hand. "About this high?"

Stiggy shrugged. "Dunno, can't remember. Does it matter?"

"Well yeah."

"You'll need to ask Mike about it then, I were out of me fucking head last night." Stiggy ran his fingers through his wet hair, then wiped them on the front of his T-shirt.

"Is it raining out?" Brian asked.

Stiggy shook his head. "No, why?"

"You're all wet."

"Yeah well, I fell in the river, didn't I?"

Brian laughed. "What, glued up again were you?"

Stiggy shook his head again. "Nah, were I fuck."

"Come off it, I can smell it from here," Colin said.

"Well, yeah, I were a bit," Stiggy said. He looked down at the table, then looked back up at Colin. "But I weren't tripping or nothing, so I knew what I were doing."

Colin caught Brian's eye and grinned at him. "So how did you end up falling in the river then?"

"Well, there were this bloke, and ..."

"What, and he pushed you in the river?" Colin tried to keep a straight face, but it wasn't easy when he saw Brian's expression.

Stiggy shook his head vigorously, sending water spraying in all directions. "Nah, he had this big sack and he chucked it in the river, I don't think he saw me at all."

"So how did you end up in the river then?" Brian asked.

Stiggy looked at Brian blankly for a few seconds before replying. "Well I thought it might be some cats, didn't I?"

"Some cats?" Colin asked.

"Yeah. It were all lumpy, like."

"Why would someone put cats in a sack and throw it in the river?"

"Oh, I don't know," Brian said, shaking his head. "There's some really cruel people about."

Colin shrugged. "Well yeah, but you'd hear them wouldn't you? The cats, I mean. They'd make a right fucking noise."

"Not if they were dead," Stiggy said.

"Well if they were dead it wouldn't really matter if they got chucked in the river would it?" Brian said. "Anyway, that still doesn't explain how you fell in."

"I were trying to get them out with a stick."

Colin leaned forward over the table. "What, the dead cats?" He grinned at Brian.

"Yeah." Stiggy nodded. "Then I went and leaned over too far, didn't I?"

"You daft cunt," Brian said. "What did you want with a sack full of dead cats anyway?"

"I didn't say they *were* dead cats, I said I thought they *might* have been cats. Could have been anything really."

"So what was in the sack then?" Colin asked.

"I don't know. I fell in the river didn't I?"

"Didn't you have a look while you were in there?"

"I never thought of that. I just wanted to get out of the water, it were fucking freezing."

Brian shook his head and sighed. "For fuck's sake."

Stiggy leaned on the table and rose to his feet, then shuffled himself out of the bucket seat. "Yeah well, I'm off to the bog. You two waiting here?"

Colin nodded. After Stiggy left Brian burst out laughing. "That guy's a fucking head case," he said.

Colin smiled and shook his head. "Nah, Stiggy's okay when you get to know him. And if anything kicks off at the Cockney Upstarts gig he'll be a good bloke to have on our side."

Brian grunted. "He's off his fucking head on glue most of the time. All that bollocks about bags of cats in the river and throwing pigs' heads at people?"

"That's just the glue talking, he's pretty sound when he's not on it. And he's a right vicious cunt in a fight, you heard what he said he did to that skinhead last night."

Brian frowned. "You think there might be some bother at the gig?"

Colin shrugged. "Dunno, maybe. They do have a big skinhead following. So the more punks who go along the better, really."

"Yeah, I guess." Brian took out his cigarettes and lit one. He blew smoke rings across the table at Colin. "He's taking his time in the bogs, what do you reckon he's doing in there?"

"Knowing him, probably getting glued up."

"What, in Woolworths? He'll get us chucked out."

Colin smiled. "Well there's only one way to find out."

* * *

"No fucking way," Brian said when he opened the toilet door and looked in.

Colin pushed past him to see for himself. Stiggy stood

before a wall-mounted hand dryer, holding his Discharge T-shirt under it. His camouflage trousers were draped over a nearby sink, dripping water onto the floor. Stiggy's socks were stuffed inside his canvas trainers, which lay by his bare feet.

"Oi, shut the fucking door, you're making a draft," Stiggy said. The dryer stopped, and he pushed a button with his forehead to restart it.

Colin closed the toilet door and stood with his back against it while Brian made his way to the urinal. Stiggy put his T-shirt on and reached for his trousers. He wrung them out in the sink and held them under the dryer.

"Aren't you going to dry your underpants?" Colin asked. Brian laughed. He looked over his shoulder from the urinal.

"I did them first," Stiggy said.

"Fucking hell," Brian said. "I'm glad we waited before coming in now. You'd have put me off me piss stood there with your arse out." He walked across to the sink and washed his hands, then splashed cold water on Stiggy's bare legs.

"Fuck off, you cunt!" Stiggy shouted.

"You what?" Brian said, flicking more water at him. "Can't hear you over the dryer."

Stiggy swung the wet trousers at Brian. Brian dodged out of the way, laughing.

"Come on Col," Brian said, "let's leave him to it. I'm off home for me tea anyway. You out tomorrow?"

Colin shook his head. "Nah, I said I'd take me Gran to the cemetery to visit me Granddad, that always ends up upsetting her so I'll probably stay in after that."

"Ah, okay. I'm helping me dad all day Friday, so I guess I'll see you at The Juggler's Rest after tea then."

Colin nodded. "Yeah. You reckon them birds will be there?"

Brian shrugged. "Don't see why not, it was their idea."

"Who's this you're on about?" Stiggy asked.

"Couple of birds we met earlier," Colin said.

"What, punk birds, you mean?"

"No, *mod* ones," Brian said. "Of course they were fucking punk birds. Who else would look twice at an ugly cunt like that?" he added, pointing at Colin.

Stiggy laughed.

"Fuck you," Colin said with a grin. "It were me they fancied."

"They felt sorry for you, more like."

"So have they got a mate then?" Stiggy asked.

* * *

Trog had finished work for the day and headed into town for a quick pint in The Black Bull. His heart sank when he saw Mandy talking to Don at the bar. The way they both fell silent, the look on Mandy's face when she caught Trog's eye. He had been hoping last night wasn't just a one-off, a mad fling on Mandy's part, but there was no smile to welcome him. It looked more like Mandy was going to tell him to fuck off.

"Trog," Mandy said. "Did you hear about Ian?"

Trog shrugged, relieved it was about something else. "Why, what's he done now?"

"He got attacked last night," Don said, "he's in a really bad way."

"What?" Trog wheeled on Don, his eyes wide.

"The coppers came for me this morning, wanting to know if I knew anything about it. They said Ian's mum gave them my address. I'm surprised they didn't go round to yours too."

"I've been at work," Trog said, "I haven't been home yet. So what happened then?"

"Dunno. He missed his bus, that was the last I saw of him. I said he could crash at mine, but he said he fancied some chips anyway so he'd walk home."

"So where is he now?"

"He's in the hospital."

"Well let's get down there, then, and find out who did it so we can fucking batter them."

"Hold on," Mandy said, "I'll close up here and come with you."

* * *

Trog stared down, open-mouthed, at the figure lying before him. Bandages covered Ian's face and upper body like an Egyptian mummy. A clear plastic tube inserted into Ian's throat pumped oxygen from a machine by his bed. An IV drip hanging beside him led to a needle taped onto his left hand. Another tube in the side of his chest drained brown fluid into a bag hanging from the side of the bed. A machine on a trolley next to the bed beeped regularly, the only sign Ian was still alive, his only movement the faint rise and fall of his chest in time with the oxygen machine's bellows.

"Fucking ... hell," Trog said. He hadn't expected anything like this.

Don slumped into a nearby chair and held his head in his hands. "Jesus fucking Christ."

Mandy shook her head slowly.

"Can I help you?" a nurse asked. Nobody had noticed her approach until she spoke.

"How is he?" Trog asked.

"Are you a relative?" the nurse asked.

"Yes, we all are," Mandy said, before Trog had a chance to reply.

The nurse smiled faintly at Mandy and shook her head. "He's not good, I'm afraid. He's got a fractured skull and two broken ribs, one of which punctured a lung. We repaired the damage, but it's the injuries to his head we are most concerned about. Until he regains consciousness we won't know if there is any long term damage."

"What, like brain damage?" Don asked. He stood up and glared at the nurse as if it was all her fault.

The nurse looked at Don and shook her head slowly. "It's too early to say. I'll get a doctor to explain it to you properly, but we'll need to run some tests when he wakes up."

"How long do you think it will take for him to wake up?" Mandy asked.

"I can't really tell you at this stage. Like I say, I'll get a doctor to…"

"How long has he been unconscious?" Trog asked.

The nurse looked at Trog, then looked away. "Since he arrived last night."

"Why is his face all bandaged up like that?" Mandy asked.

The nurse's face paled. She shook her head. "It was a very savage attack. Whoever did this cut his face up pretty bad. He…" Her voice faltered when she caught the cold glare of the two skinheads. She looked away before continuing. "He'll need reconstructive surgery further down the line. Now if you'll excuse me, I need to check on another patient. I'll send a doctor to talk to you."

"Jesus fucking Christ," Don repeated after the nurse left. "So what now?"

Trog leaned over Ian's prone figure and shook his head. "I don't know, Don. But some cunt is going to fucking pay for this."

"Yeah but until he comes round we won't know who did it."

"Someone will know," Trog said. "I'm going to find out who did this. And when I do I'm going to fucking kill them."

3 Reality Asylum

Colin's grandmother hadn't been as upset about the visit to his grandfather's grave as he expected, so after they got home Colin checked she was still okay to be left, and when she assured him she was, he got a bus into town. Nobody was in any of the regular hangouts, so he made his way to Stiggy's bedsit on the outskirts of town.

It was right in the heart of the local red light area, and as soon as Colin entered the street he was approached by a middle-aged woman in a low-cut black top and PVC miniskirt. She had sunken, staring eyes, accentuated rather than hidden by her liberal use of makeup. She scratched her left arm and picked at a scab.

"Are you looking for business?"

Colin felt his face flush. He shook his head slowly and walked past without speaking.

"Fuck you then," she shouted after him.

Colin entered Stiggy's front yard and squeezed past a broken washing machine to reach the front door. It opened without a key and he stepped into a communal hall. The boom boom boom of a heavy dub reggae bassline seeped through the door of Flat One as he passed. Colin walked up to Flat Two and knocked on the door.

"Who is it?" Stiggy shouted from behind the door a few seconds later.

"It's me, Colin."

The door opened a tiny crack and Stiggy peered out. He grinned and opened the door fully. "All right, Col? What you doing here?"

"All right, Stiggy. Just thought I'd come and see you."

Damp, decay and stale glue wafted out of the dingy room. Stiggy stood to one side and Colin squeezed between him and an old armchair just behind the door. Inside, taking up most of one wall, was a small unmade bed with no headboard, a single brown blanket strewn across it in a rumpled heap.

Stiggy sat down in the armchair and toyed with a tuft of stuffing hanging out of one of the arms. Colin looked around and sat on the edge of the bed, leaning forward with his hands on his knees. Opposite him was an unvarnished wooden chest of drawers with a battered old music centre perched on top of it. A few dog-eared records stood next to it, propped up by a haphazard pile of hand-written cassettes.

On the wall above the music centre, surrounded by peeling off-white paint, was a black and white poster of a severed hand caught on barbed wire bearing the slogan 'Your country needs you.' Colin guessed from the criss-cross of regularly spaced creases it had probably come free with one of Stiggy's records. The floor of the room was covered by a threadbare carpet that had once had a vibrant pattern weaved into it, but was now just a dingy brown colour, stained and caked in mud and assorted spillages that hadn't been cleaned up over the years.

Stiggy drummed his fingers on the arms of the chair, completely out of step with the thumping reggae bass-line coming through the wall. "I got the new Discharge album the other day if you want to hear it?" he said, jumping up. He walked over to the music centre and switched it on.

"Not really," Colin said. "They're just a load of noise."

Stiggy grunted as he lifted a cracked Perspex lid up on its hinges. "Are they fuck. What about this one then? They're new."

Stiggy turned around and held up a red and black single sleeve. Colin stood up and moved closer, then tilted his head to read the band name printed down the side.

"Varukers? Never heard of them, what are they like?"

"They're fucking smart mate," Stiggy said, pulling out the record and placing it on the turntable. He flipped a switch and sat down in the armchair. When the music started he tapped his foot rapidly to it and mouthed some of the words.

Colin frowned. They sounded even worse than Discharge. He scooped up Stiggy's records and took them back to the bed, then spread them out before him. Most of them were by bands he had never heard of, and he wondered where Stiggy had bought them from. Colin certainly hadn't seen any of them in the local record shop.

"Haven't you got any Cockney Upstarts records?"

Stiggy shook his head. "Nah, they're shite."

"Well if you don't like them why are you coming to Shefferham with us?"

Stiggy shrugged. "I want to see them throw a pig's head at a skinhead. It'll be a laugh. Anyway there's nowt else to do, is there?"

Colin smiled and shook his head. How could anyone be so gullible they would believe what they read in a newspaper? According to newspapers, punks liked to spit on old grannies and stuck safety pins through practically every part of their body. Nothing could be further from the truth.

Stiggy stood up and walked over to the bed. He pointed at one of the singles. "That one's good," he said.

Colin picked up the cheaply-printed wraparound record sleeve and peered at it. A black and white screaming face stared out at him, surrounded by seemingly random images. He tilted it to read the stencilled lettering around the face, then flipped it over. A punk sat before a pile of dead bodies. He unfolded the cover to see what was printed inside, and a Crass single fell out. Colin picked the record up and folded the sleeve around it. He shook his head and tossed it back onto the bed.

"I don't like Crass," he said.

Stiggy leaned over and picked up the single. "It's not by

Crass, it's just on their record label. Like Flux of Pink Indians was."

Colin looked up at Stiggy and nodded. "Oh, okay."

Colin had been surprised when he first heard Tube Disasters at one of Twiglet's parties and been told it was by a Crass band. He had bought a Crass single once, on a whim because it was very cheap. He hated it. There had been no tune to it whatsoever, just a noise with some woman ranting about Jesus. Colin didn't bother playing the other side, he just threw it in the bin and vowed never to buy anything by Crass ever again, no matter how cheap it was or how many people said how great the band was.

"They've got an album coming out soon," Stiggy said, putting the record on the turntable. "I bet it'll be fucking great."

While the song played, Colin looked through the other records spread over Stiggy's bed. He didn't care much for the single's title song, it was too slow and ponderous for his tastes, but he did like the more upbeat B side even though its lyrics were somewhat depressing.

Colin made a mental note to ask Stiggy to tape it for him once he got his cassette player fixed. A Ramones tape Brian made for him a few weeks earlier had got caught up in the mechanism and was now inextricably wound up inside it, having snapped off when Colin tried to pull it loose. He would need to take a screwdriver to the cassette player and open it up to get the remaining tape out, a job he wasn't particularly looking forward to.

Colin picked out a few more records for Stiggy to play. The Tube Disasters EP, singles by Anti Pasti and The Exploited he was already familiar with, and a few others he chose because their sleeves looked interesting. After playing them, Stiggy picked up an album by Crass with what looked like a blow up sex doll on the cover.

"Oh fuck off, do you have to put that shit on?" Colin

asked, shaking his head.

"Yeah, I want something a bit longer." Stiggy unfolded the cover and took out the record to put it on the turntable. Colin sighed and shuffled further onto the bed so he could lean his back against the wall. He decided the next time he went to Stiggy's bedsit he would take some of his own records along with him, show Stiggy what he was missing out on.

While the woman on the Crass album screeched through the first song, Stiggy pulled open a drawer and took out a roll of sandwich bags and a half-litre can of Evo Stik. He tore a bag from the roll and held it out to Colin.

Colin smiled. "Don't tell Brian," he said, and leaned forward to take the bag.

Stiggy shook his head and smirked. He tore off another bag and rolled down its edges, then balanced it on his knee while he poured a large dollop of glue into one of the corners. He passed the can to Colin and breathed into the bag, massaging the glue-filled corner between his index finger and thumb. His eyes glazed over.

Colin poured a small amount of glue into the bag and lifted it to his mouth. He glanced over at Stiggy as he took a few tentative breaths, saw he was already away with the fairies. He thought about ditching the glue-bag, hiding it under Stiggy's bedcovers. Stiggy wouldn't know any different. Then he decided to take a few more breaths, just to see what the attraction was.

Colin closed his eyes and sighed, concentrating on the rustling sound the plastic bag made as it inflated and deflated. It seemed to echo, sounding impossibly loud. Crass echoed too. Their music darted around the room like hummingbirds looking for an escape from Stiggy's bedsit, the screaming woman chasing them with a buzzing chainsaw. Crass seemed so much better than Colin remembered them being before. Maybe it was because the hummingbirds taught them how to play?

As if they had somehow heard Colin's thoughts, Crass decided they were going home and left behind just a regular ka-thunk ka-thunk ka-thunk ka-thunk ka-thunk as the hummingbirds pecked away at Colin's skull.

Colin opened his eyes. Stiggy stood before him, waving his arms around in a blur. Long yellow teeth stretched down from Stiggy's mouth and curled around his chin. The hummingbirds scattered away with a flutter. Stiggy's teeth retreated back into his mouth.

"You have a good one?" Stiggy asked.

Colin looked around him, unsure of his location. He shook his head. "Fucking ... hell," he said. He handed Stiggy the dried up glue-bag and glanced at a clock by the side of the bed. An hour had passed that he had no memory of. The Crass record had finished long ago, the record player's stylus stuck in its lead-out groove. Stiggy walked over and lifted the tone arm, silencing it with a loud thrrrrup. He lifted the record and flipped it over, put it back on the turntable.

"You want some cider?" Stiggy asked over the jangling guitar intro. "It'll keep you buzzed longer."

Colin shook his head. "Nah, I feel a bit wrecked as it is, so I reckon I'll just get off home."

"You sure? Glue makes you crash if you don't top it up with booze."

"Nah, you're all right. I'll get a can of beer from home or something if I need to."

Stiggy shrugged. "Fair enough. See you at The Juggler's Rest tomorrow then, yeah?"

Outside, the prostitute approached Colin again and asked if he was looking for business. Colin smiled and shook his head.

"No, sorry."

4 It's All Done by Mirrors

Colin leaned against a wall outside The Juggler's Rest while he waited for Brian to arrive. He looked down at Stiggy, who sat on the pavement by his side, breathing into a glue-bag. Colin didn't know how Stiggy had the nerve to do it right there, out in the open where anyone could see.

"Look at my shoes!" Stiggy shouted. Fucking hell, look at my shoes!" His eyes were wide and staring, and the glue-bag flopped around in his hands as he gestured wildly at his trainers.

"Yeah, very nice," Colin said.

Stiggy raised the bag to his mouth and spoke into it, still staring at his trainers. "My shoes have got magical powers. Why didn't anyone tell me?"

Colin sighed and shook his head, wondering if that was what he had been like himself at Stiggy's bedsit the previous day. He reached into his leather jacket pocket for his cigarettes, and was about to light one when he thought about the solvent fumes in the air around him. He didn't know if they would be flammable or not, so he decided to be cautious and took several steps away from Stiggy first. He took a deep drag and looked down the empty street. No sign of Brian yet, and he was already fifteen minutes late. No sign of the girls either.

He turned his attention to a poster displayed in the window of The Juggler's Rest. A hand-drawn, simplistic doodle of a nun brandishing a crucifix in a suggestive manner advertised the evening's entertainment. Welwyn Garden City's pranksters in revolt The Astronauts present an evening of folk in hell, it promised. All for an entrance fee of just fifty pence. The poster didn't inspire Colin with confidence, and if Becky and Kaz hadn't said they would be going he would've given it a miss and gone to The White Swan instead.

"All right, Col!"

Colin turned away from the poster. Brian strode toward him, his leather jacket flapping open in the wind to reveal an Exploited T-shirt beneath it.

"About fucking time," Colin said. "We've been here ages."

"Yeah well, I'm here now aren't I?" Brian pointed at Stiggy. "What the fuck's he doing here? Talk about fucking gooseberries."

"Never mind Stiggy, what's that fucking stink?"

Colin leaned closer to Brian and sniffed. A flowery, chemical smell mixed with tobacco smoke assaulted his nostrils, so potent he could almost taste it in his mouth. He wafted his hand under his nose in an attempt to disperse it, but the smell lingered, overpowering him.

"Borrowed a dab of me dad's aftershave, didn't I?" Brian said. "Got to make an effort now and again, haven't you?"

"Smells like you used the whole fucking bottle."

Brian grunted. "Any sign of them birds yet?"

"Not seen them."

"You checked inside?"

"No, you have to pay to get in tonight. There's a band on."

Brian looked at the poster in the window. "An evening of folk? Sounds crap."

Colin smiled. "Yeah. When them birds get here I reckon we should fuck off somewhere else with them."

"Yeah, maybe. Let's go see if they're inside. If not, fuck it. We'll wait half an hour, then get our money back and go down The White Swan."

Colin gestured at Stiggy, who was mumbling something into his glue-bag. "What about him?"

"Just leave him there, he'll not know any different when he's in that state."

"Yeah, but what if some coppers see him?"

Brian shrugged. "Who cares?"

"Nah, I think we'd best take him with us. You hold his arms while I get the glue off him. They'll not let him in with that."

* * *

Just inside the doorway, a man dressed in black sat behind a small table.

"Evening, lads," the man said. He picked up a lidless Quality Street tin and rattled loose change around in it. "Fifty pence to get in."

Brian put a fifty pence coin down on the table and pushed through a door into the bar. Stiggy followed him without paying. The man looked at Colin.

"Fifty pence each, that is. You paying for your mate then?"

Colin sighed and shrugged. He unzipped his leather jacket pocket, took out a pound note and handed it to the man, then followed Brian and Stiggy into the bar.

A few local punks and older hippies sat around small tables placed in front of a make-shift stage area near the toilets. A tall, thin man with long hair threaded cables across the carpet and taped them down, getting everything ready for the band. Colin nodded to a few people he recognised and headed for the bar to join Brian.

"Any sign of them birds yet?" Brian asked.

Colin shook his head. "Not seen them. Where's Stiggy?"

"He went in the bogs, probably getting glued up again. He'd better not get us chucked out before we get our money back."

The barman approached and they ordered a pint each, then took them in search of a spare table to sit at so they could watch the entrance door. They skirted around the long-haired man in the stage area, who was positioning a microphone stand to the right of a small drum kit. All the tables immediately in front of the stage area were full, so Colin and Brian headed into a small secluded area in the corner. Becky and Kaz sat there, sipping from glasses of Pernod and blackcurrant. They both smiled and waved.

"All right. Been here long?" Colin asked. He put his pint down on the table and sat down opposite Becky.

"No, not really," Becky said. She sat up straight in her chair and pulled down her pink mohair jumper to smooth out invisible creases. Colin stared at her green fishnet stockings and nodded absentmindedly.

"Budge up," Brian said, and squeezed himself between Becky and Kaz. "You fancy getting off somewhere else after this?"

Kaz shook her head. "No, we want to see the band. We've never been to a gig before, and we already paid to get in."

"What, never?" Colin asked. "How come?"

Kaz shrugged and looked away.

"Kaz's dad won't let her," Becky said, "he says it's too dangerous. He'd have a fit if he knew she was here."

"That's just daft," Colin said. "We've been to loads and we've never seen any trouble."

"So far," Brian said.

* * *

"What the fuck are we doing here?" Don asked, looking at a crude drawing of a nun in the window of The Juggler's Rest.

"There's a fucking punk gig on tonight," Trog said. "Word is that student cunt I battered the other night will be there and I want to have a word with him, see if he knows anything about Ian."

"What, you reckon it was him that did Ian over?"

Trog laughed. "Nah. He's all talk that one, but he might know who did. Here, did I tell you he pissed himself when he saw me?"

Don looked at Trog and smiled. "Yeah?"

"Yeah, straight up. He turned round, saw me, then fucking pissed his pants."

Don shook his head and laughed. "Mate, I wish I'd been there to see that. Fucking hell, what a classic. Come on then, let's go and see what the cunt's got to say for himself."

* * *

"That's the cunt there," Trog said, pointing from the bar. "The one with the bleached sticky-up hair, looks life a fucking scarecrow. That's his mate, he's probably weak as piss too."

Don nodded and took a sip of lager. "The bogs'll probably be our best bet. More secluded, less chance of being interrupted by the other yetis."

While Don spoke, the student punk turned and locked eyes with Trog. He stared for a few seconds, open-mouthed, then looked away.

"You see that?" Trog asked. "The fucking cunt just gave me a right look."

"Fuck him," Don said, "he'll get his soon enough."

* * *

The long-haired roadie finished setting up the band's equipment and picked up a Sainsbury's carrier bag that was propped up against a wall behind the drum-kit. He reached inside and pulled out a twelve inch record with a black and red cover, then walked up to the nearest table with it. He leaned over to talk to the people sitting there, a pair of hippies in their late twenties, and when one of them nodded he handed over the record and took some money for it. He moved on to the next table.

"Anyone want to buy an album?" the man asked when he reached Colin's table. He held one out for them to see. Its stark black and red cover image showed two stencilled figures, a businessman and a court jester, staring at each other across a diagonal divide.

Colin read the lettering printed around the edges of the record sleeve and saw it was by The Astronauts, the band who were playing later. He took the album from the man and flipped it over to look at the song titles printed on the back. The first track was something about seagulls, the second a Dixieland blues song.

"Nah, you're all right, mate," Colin said, shaking his head, and put the record down on the table.

Becky leaned forward and picked it up. "How much are they?" she asked.

"Three pounds," the long-haired man said.

"Giz a look then," Brian said, and snatched the record from Becky's hand. Kaz leaned over to look at it with him.

"You want to buy one?" the man asked.

Brian shrugged and handed him the record back. "Nah, not really."

"Okay, fair enough. Catch you later, yeah?" The man turned and walked away to try his luck at the next table.

Colin finished off his beer and looked toward the bar. The two skinheads were still standing there, staring at him. One made a gun from his fingers and pointed it at Colin, then raised it to his mouth and blew imaginary smoke from it. Colin looked away.

"You want another drink?" he asked Becky. Becky smiled and nodded. Colin turned to Brian. "Get the drinks in, yeah? I'm just off to the bog." He took out two pound notes and gave them to Brian.

Brian sighed, then rose to his feet. "You coming to help me carry them, Kaz?"

"See you in a bit," Colin said, nodding to Becky.

Stiggy stumbled out of the toilet door just as Colin approached it, and staggered toward the bar. Colin went inside, frowned at a strong smell of solvents, and headed for one of the two cubicle toilets. After his experience in The Queen's Head he didn't want to take any chances, and bolted the door behind him.

He lifted up the seat and urinated into the toilet with a sigh. He zipped up and wiped his hands on his trousers, then slid back the bolt and opened the cubicle door.

The two skinheads scowled in at him from the doorway.

Blood rushed to Colin's face. The earth lurched beneath him. He reached out for the cubicle wall to steady himself and gasped for air. His eyes darted from one skinhead to the other.

"What do you want?" Colin's voice came out with a squeak.

One of the skinheads, the short one who had attacked him in The Queen's Head, took a step forward. "What do you know about our mate?" he asked in a gruff voice.

Colin took an involuntary step back and felt the toilet bowl press against the back of his legs. The short skinhead stepped into the cubicle. The taller one stood guard in the doorway, staring in. Colin wondered what his chances of pushing past them both and escaping back into the bar would be.

"Er ... you what?" Colin asked.

The skinhead grabbed Colin's leather jacket and pulled him out of the cubicle. Colin lost his footing and stumbled. The skinhead held him tight, pulled him back to his feet and dragged him across the toilet. He swung Colin around to face him, pressed him up against a wall, and raised a fist. It hovered before Colin's face, ready to strike.

"I said, what do you know about our fucking mate?"

The taller skinhead stood behind him, a look of fury on his face. He clenched his fists and puffed out his chest, his eyes blazing.

Colin felt his knees weaken. His hands shook when he held them out before him.

"Look, I, um ..."

"Well?" the short skinhead asked, and pulled back his fist.

Colin flinched and closed his eyes. "I don't know nothing," he said, quickly. When no blow came he opened his eyes. "Why, what's happened?"

"One of our mates got done over. We think you know something about it."

Colin shook his head. "Look, I ..." He swallowed hard to clear his dry throat. "I don't know nothing about it, honest. It wasn't me."

The short skinhead laughed. "Yeah, I guessed that. But I reckon you know who did do it, and I want you to tell me. Now!" He pulled back his fist again.

"Look, mate ..." Colin began, holding up his hands. He heard the toilet door open and looked toward it. Brian and Stiggy stood in the doorway, looking in.

"You all right there, Col?" Brian asked.

The two skinheads looked around. The short one released Colin and stepped away from him. They both turned to face Brian and Stiggy, their fists clenched by their sides. Colin sidestepped away from them.

"Is there a problem?" Brian asked, looking at Colin.

The two skinheads looked from Brian and Stiggy to Colin and back, then glanced at each other. The short one shook his head slowly.

"No problem here, mate. We were just having a chat, weren't we?" He glared at Colin.

"Is that right?" Brian asked. Colin shrugged.

Brian walked up to the urinal, keeping his eyes firmly on the two skinheads the whole time. Stiggy stayed by the exit, and when the two skinheads walked toward him he held the door open for them.

"Fucking yeti," the taller skinhead said under his breath as they left. Stiggy let the door close behind them.

"What was all that about?" Brian asked.

Colin shrugged. "They said one of their mates got done over, they wanted to know if I knew who did it."

"You didn't tell them, did you?" Stiggy asked. He looked at the closed toilet door.

"Nah, did I fuck. But I don't think they'll let it go, so you'd best watch your back from now on. And don't go bragging about it to anyone else."

* * *

Colin turned to face the stage area when he heard a high-pitched whine of feedback. The long-haired man tapped his fingers on a microphone. A guitarist tuned up, while a bass player crouched down to adjust dials on a small amplifier. The drummer sat behind his drum kit, drinking from a bottle of lager.

"One two, one two," the long haired man said.

Someone from the audience, a local punk with ripped purple trousers and an unruly mess of purple hair to match, strode up to the stage area.

"Go on, Marco," a female voice shouted from one of the tables near the stage.

The youth said something to the long-haired man, who smiled in return and gestured at the microphone. The youth grabbed the microphone's stand, tilted it toward himself, and scowled at the audience.

"Fuck Thatcher," he shouted. "You took us into this fucking war but nobody knows what we're fighting for some fucking sheep some fucking land what the fuck do we want that for you fucking skank you fucking—"

He continued shouting for several minutes, to the accompaniment of blasts of feedback and an occasional beat on the drums. As one poem ended he started another before anyone could react, until with a final scream he walked off the stage and retook his seat.

"Well I hope the band is better than that," Brian said.

"I thought he was cute," Becky said, smiling. She craned her neck to see where the youth had gone.

The long-haired man tapped on the microphone again. "Right. Hello, I think we might be ready to start now. I'll just take my pullover off, it's a bit hot in here."

"Fucking hippy," someone shouted from the bar. Colin smiled and looked to see who it was, and saw the two skinheads standing there. His heart sank. He nudged Brian and nodded to them. Brian turned to look.

"Thank you for that contribution," the long-haired man said. He smiled and flicked his hair back over his shoulder with a jerk of his head.

"Don't worry about it," Brian said, "they'll not do anything with this many people here."

"What are you on about?" Kaz asked, looking at the bar.

"Nothing," Brian said. "Let's watch the band."

"Right. Okay," the long-haired man said. "Well I'm Mark and we're The Astronauts, and we sound a bit like this." He counted in the band, adding emphasis to the final digit. "One two three four, one two three *four*."

* * *

Trog turned his back on the band when they started to play. He clapped his hand on Don's shoulder to get his attention and leaned over to shout into his ear.

"I still reckon that student cunt knows something about it."

Don nodded. "Yeah, so do I. Not much we can do about it tonight though, just the two of us, so we might as well get fucked off. This fucking hippy music's doing me head in anyway."

Trog picked up his lager and drained the glass. He turned and watched the singer cavorting around the microphone stand like some demented ballerina. He turned back to Don and put the empty pint glass down on the bar.

"Yeah, drink up then. Hopefully Ian will come round soon, and he can tell us who it was. Then we'll get a fucking army together and do the cunt proper."

Don drained his glass in one go and belched. He thumped the glass down on the bar and walked away. Trog took a final look at the band, shook his head, and followed

Don through the door.

* * *

The music took Colin by surprise. From the long hair of the singer, and the promise of folk music on the poster outside, he had expected something like Pink Floyd or one of those other ghastly bands of that ilk, and had been ready to walk out as soon as they started. But while being a lot more melodic than Colin's usual taste in music, the songs were certainly catchy and the tales of urban decay told by the lyrics were definitely something he could relate to.

Colin looked at Brian, intending to ask if he wanted to get up and dance with him. Brian had his arm around Kaz's shoulder. He turned to face her and shouted something into her ear. Kaz smiled and shouted something back. Colin sighed and nudged Stiggy.

"Come on, Stiggy."

Stiggy looked at Colin, but remained seated until Colin pulled him to his feet and dragged him by the arm into the midst of a few punks who were shuffling around before the band. He let him go, then swung his arms and jumped about in time to the music. Stiggy caught the back of Colin's hand across his face when he didn't move out of the way in time, and shoulder-barged Colin in retaliation. Stiggy kicked out his feet and leaped around, flailing his arms at anyone who got too close to him. Colin kept his distance, having seen Stiggy dance lots of times before and not wanting to get any fresh bruises to go with the ones he already had.

A few songs later, Colin's energy started to sag. He squeezed his way out of the make-shift dance area and returned to his seat. He sat down and lifted the front of his T-shirt to wipe sweat from his face, then took a long drink to cool himself down.

"I can see how you got your bruises now," Becky shouted. "Do you always dance like that?"

"Yeah. Why, what's up with it?"

Becky smiled. "Nothing. So what do you think of the band then? Glad you came?"

Colin nodded. "Yeah, they're pretty good. I wish I'd bought that record now."

Colin turned to watch the band. Stiggy was still jumping around haphazardly, lurching into the other punks and sending them stumbling away from him with his fists.

The band announced their final song, and three minutes later it was all over. Dancers drifted away from the stage area, bruised and happy. Some headed for the bar, others returned to their seats and made ready to go home. Stiggy went into the toilet.

Becky stood up and approached the stage area, then spoke to the singer. He bent down to listen, nodded, and reached for the bag of records. He pulled one out and handed it to Becky. Becky paid him and returned to Colin.

"Here you go," she said, smiling.

"Er ... thanks," Colin said, and took the record from her.

Becky stood before him and swung her shoulders. She smiled. "Buy me a drink?"

"Er ... yeah, sure." Colin looked to the bar, expecting the two skinheads to still be there. But all he saw was a smattering of punks and a few old hippies. "What do you want?"

"Pernod and black."

* * *

Stiggy lurched out of the toilet and staggered toward Colin's table. He stumbled into the back of a chair and looked down. The chair's occupant turned and glared at him. Stiggy shrugged and carried on walking, then came to a swaying halt. He looked around, seemingly lost. Colin waved to get his attention. Stiggy nodded and veered off in the right direction. He flopped into his chair and picked up his half-empty glass of cider, then looked over the rim at Colin.

"What?" Stiggy asked.

Colin laughed. "Nothing, mate. We thought you'd gone home."

Stiggy put down the glass and tapped his chest. "No, not yet," he said, shaking his head.

Colin laughed. Brian and Becky did too. Stiggy looked at them with a puzzled expression.

"What?" Stiggy repeated.

Colin smiled and shook his head. "Nothing, mate." He picked up the record and showed it to Stiggy. "Here, look what Becky bought me."

Stiggy cocked his head to one side as he looked at it. "What is it?"

"A record. It's by that band that were just on."

Stiggy blinked and rubbed his eyes with his fists. "Yeah? Can you tape it for me?"

Colin shook his head and put the record back down on the table. He took out a cigarette and lit it. "I can't mate, me tape recorder's broke. But I can borrow you it if you want? Then you can tape it for Brian as well."

Stiggy nodded. "Yeah, cheers."

"I'll fetch it round to your bedsit tomorrow afternoon, we can do it before we go to Shefferham."

"Why, what's in Shefferham?" Becky asked.

"Cockney Upstarts are playing," Brian said. "We're all going down there on the train." He turned to Kaz. "You fancy it? It should be a good one."

Kaz frowned. "No, my dad won't let me. Anyway, I don't like skinhead bands, and I don't think *you* should go either. It won't be safe."

Brian shook his head. "Nah, there's loads of us going, we'll be okay. Anyway they're not a skinhead band."

"Do you have to go?" Kaz put her hand on Brian's chest and stared into his eyes.

Brian shrugged. "Well yeah. They're from that London,

they don't come down here very often so it'll probably be the only chance we get to see them."

Kaz frowned again. She leaned back and folded her arms over her chest, glowering at Brian. Brian looked away and toyed with his half-empty beer glass. Kaz sighed and turned to Becky. "I need a wee. Are you coming, Becky?"

Becky smiled. "Yeah okay." She turned to Colin. "You'll wait for us, won't you?"

Colin nodded. He grinned at Brian and took a drag on his cigarette. "I need a *wee wee*, are you coming Brian?" he said in a high pitched voice, mimicking Kaz.

Kaz glared at Colin and stamped off, arm in arm with Becky. Brian sniggered, and took a long drink from his beer. He belched at Colin and rose to his feet. "Come on then. But no peeping at me cock."

"Fuck off," Colin said, and turned to Stiggy. "You watch our stuff for us?"

Stiggy nodded and picked up the record.

In the toilet, Brian and Colin took up positions either side of the urinal. Colin threw his cigarette end into the middle and it landed in the water with a hiss. He aimed his urine at it, pushing it toward Brian. Brian smiled and aimed his penis to push it back, shuffling closer to Colin for a better aim. Colin's bladder emptied first and his urine turned to dribbles while Brian's was still in full flow. The sodden cigarette end hit Colin's end of the urinal and Brian bellowed in victory.

"Cheating bastard," Colin said, zipping up.

Back in the bar, Stiggy was reading the song titles from the back of the record sleeve when Colin approached him from behind.

"Have they gone?" Colin asked, looking around the pub. Most of the other customers had already left.

"Have what gone?" Stiggy asked without looking up from the record cover.

"Becky and Kaz."

"Who?"

Colin sighed. "Them birds you've been sitting with all night."

Stiggy shrugged. "Still in the bogs, aren't they? What time is it anyway?"

Brian looked at his watch. "Half-ten."

"What?" Stiggy looked up at Brian, wide-eyed. He dropped the record on the table and stood up. "I've got to go. See you tomorrow night at the train station."

After Stiggy rushed out, Brian looked at Colin and shrugged. Colin looked over at the women's toilet door. "What do you reckon they're doing in there?"

"How the fuck should I know?" Brian said. "Probably escaped out the window so they don't need to look at your ugly mug any more."

"Fuck off."

Brian laughed. "Well whatever they're doing they'd better hurry up or we'll miss the bus home."

They lit a cigarette each and smoked them. Becky and Kaz were still in the toilet when they stubbed them out. Colin looked at the toilet door and sighed. "Fuck this," he said, and rose to his feet. He banged on the door with his fist. "Oi Becky, are you in there?"

A muffled voice answered him. "Yeah, won't be long."

Colin looked at Brian, who tapped his watch with his index finger. Colin shrugged and pushed open the door.

Becky and Kaz stood before a large mirror, dabbing their faces with balls of cotton wool. Colin watched them from the doorway for a few seconds, then asked what they were doing.

Kaz looked up at Colin's reflection in the mirror. "Oi get out, you can't come in here," she said.

Colin slid through the door and let it close behind him. "Too late, I already did."

Becky smiled and continued wiping her cheek with a cotton wool ball. Kaz spun to face Colin. "Get out," she said, pointing at the door.

Colin looked around the spotlessly clean toilet with amazement. The place smelled of flowery perfume instead of shit and piss, and there wasn't even any graffiti on the walls. He watched Becky's reflection in the mirror, and when he caught her eye she smiled back at him.

"Are you going to be long?" Colin asked. "Only me and Brian need to go for the bus soon."

"Come on Becky," Kaz said. She brushed past Colin and left through the door.

Becky dropped a cotton wool ball into the sink and turned to face Colin. She leaned back against the sink with her hands, her chest pushed out.

"Do we need to go right now?" she asked, looking into Colin's eyes.

"Yeah," Colin said. He turned to the door and followed Kaz through it.

* * *

Outside on the street, Brian held his arms out straight before him and moaned, "Urrrrrrrrrrhhhhhhhh." He held his head at an angle, his mouth gaping open, and shambled up to Kaz like a zombie.

Colin put the record inside his leather jacket and tucked a corner into his jeans. He zipped his jacket up and raised his own arms, then lumbered after Becky.

"They're coming to get you, Rebecca," he said in a drawn out, gormless-sounding voice mimicking a character from an old black and white film he had watched on TV.

Becky squealed and grabbed Kaz's hand. They ran down the street together, twin pairs of monkey boots clattering down the pavement. They kept glancing behind them at Colin and Brian, who shambled after them. Their loud moans drew attention from a group of trendies passing by on the other side of the road.

"SID'S DEAD!" one shouted.

Colin gave them a two-finger salute and continued following Becky, who had stopped with Kaz a short distance away. Brian moaned again as he staggered up to Kaz. He grabbed her around the waist and made a chomping sound against her back. Kaz jerked her head to one side and screamed. Brian jolted away and clamped his hand over his ear.

"Ahhh, I've gone deaf," he cried.

"What?" Colin asked.

"I've gone deaf."

"What?"

"I've gone ... oh, fuck off, you cunt."

"Poor Brian," Kaz said, laughing, and looped her arm through his. They walked down the road together.

Colin glanced at Becky and followed them.

* * *

At the bus station they all sat on a long, wooden bench while they waited for Kaz and Becky's bus to arrive. The girls lived in a different suburb to Colin and Brian, and their bus was due to arrive a few minutes before their own. Brian and Kaz held hands and chatted away to each other.

Colin sat next to Becky and looked down at his shoes. He wondered if Becky would punch him in the face if he tried to kiss her, and decided it wasn't worth the risk. He looked up at her. She smiled and brushed against him with her shoulder. Colin bit his lip and looked away.

The bus arrived with a hiss of hydraulic brakes. Becky and Kaz jumped up and walked over to it. Colin and Brian waved goodbye and started to shuffle off to their own bus stop. Becky stepped in front of Colin, threw her arms around his neck, and kissed him on the lips. Colin winced when she crushed the cut on his lip, but the surge of emotion coursing through him as he tasted the Pernod, blackcurrant, and cheese and onion crisps on her tongue sent his head reeling. He raised his arms to return the embrace, but as suddenly as she appeared, Becky was gone. She sidestepped his grasping hands and jumped onto the bus after Kaz.

Colin watched as they stomped their way across the bus to the back seat. He waved idiotically while they blew kisses through the back window as the bus pulled out from the station.

"We should have got on that bus with them," he said to Brian when the bus disappeared from view.

"It's the last one, how would we get back home?"

Colin shrugged. He felt like he was walking on air. "What would that matter?"

He was still grinning two hours later, lying in bed wide awake and bursting with energy while a record played quietly in the background. It was the Cockney Upstarts gig tomorrow night, and he would be seeing Becky in town in the afternoon, so it looked like it was going to be the perfect day.

5 I'm an Upstart

Colin leaned against the side of a Moon Cresta machine in the train station buffet and watched Brian perform a docking manoeuvre to join two spaceships together. Brian jabbed the fire button and waggled the joystick from side to side, his movement becoming more frantic as the ships got closer together. He banked too far to the left, and one of the spaceships exploded in a ball of pixelated flames. Brian swore and thumped his fist down on the control panel.

"All right, Col," Stiggy said from the doorway.

Colin looked around and raised a hand. Brian continued playing the Moon Cresta game, frowning while he tried to avoid multi-coloured blobs falling diagonally across the screen directly at his remaining spaceship. Stiggy looked over Brian's shoulder, sighed, and sat down at a nearby table.

"I thought you said there was loads of people going?" Stiggy asked.

"They're not here yet," Colin said. "Shouldn't be long though. I think they were going to the football this afternoon, maybe they had extra time or something. The train's late anyway."

As if in confirmation, the train station tannoy announced the next train to Shefferham would be approximately twenty-three minutes late.

When Brian finished his game, he and Colin joined Stiggy at the table. They both lit cigarettes. Stiggy frowned and wafted smoke away from his face.

Ten minutes later Twiglet and Spazzo arrived, along with another youth dressed in casual gear that Colin didn't recognise. Colin looked toward the door, and when nobody else entered he asked where Mike was.

"He got nicked down at the footie, didn't he?" Twiglet

said with a shrug as he sat down at the table. "The daft cunt only went and nutted a fucking copper."

"What did he do that for?" Brian asked.

"Pissed up, weren't he? Anyway, all of a sudden there was loads of fucking coppers everywhere lashing out at anyone who stood still long enough. The rest of us fucked off sharpish and melted into the crowd."

"Aye," Spazzo said, running his fingers through his bristly green hair. "Mike got a right fucking smack round the head, split it right open. Next thing there's three of the bastards on top of him and more of the cunts running toward us with their truncheons out. Fucking mental, it were."

* * *

Trog looked up at a black and white display hanging over platform 3B and frowned.

"The fucking train's late," he said.

Don stood by the edge of the platform, bent over with his hands on his knees. He gasped for breath, having run up the stairs from the subway under the train station. He coughed, and spat a glob of mucus between his feet.

"Just as ... fucking well or we'd have ... missed the cunt."

Trog looked at Don and hitched up his bleached jeans. "Mate, you're out of fucking condition. We've only been running a few minutes."

Don straightened up and stretched his arms out behind him. He reached into his flight jacket pocket for a pack of cigarettes. "Yeah well, looks like that were a waste of fucking effort anyway."

Trog hooked his thumbs in his pockets and polished the toes of his boots on the back of his legs, one after the other.

A bored-sounding male voice, adding unnecessary emphasis to random words, made an announcement over the tannoy.

"The *next* train to arrive at platform *3B* will be the late *running* eighteen-*thirty* service to Shefferham. We *apologise* for the late *arrival* of this train, which is now due to arrive in *Shefferham* at nineteen-fifty-*five* approximately. Passengers are *advised* that the *smoking* carriage is at the rear of this train, and smoking in any *other* area of the train is not permitted. Platform *3B* for the late running eighteen-thirty *service* to Shefferham."

"There you go," Trog said, "looks like we're just in time."

A group of punks wandered out of the buffet. The gobby student, his two mates, and a couple more Trog hadn't seen before. With them was someone he knew from work.

"All right, Johnno?" Trog called out. "You off to the Cockney Upstarts then?"

"Aye up, Trog," Johnno said, nodding. "Yeah, Spazzo here were going on about it at the footie, it sounds a right laugh. So how's it going then? I haven't seen you in the showers for a while."

"I've been working the afternoon shift."

"Yeah? Can't say I'm looking forward to that myself, I reckon I might put in for permanent days when I turn eighteen."

Trog smiled. "Yeah, you and thousands others. It's not so bad really, you finish just in time for the pubs opening. It's the night shift that's the real killer."

"Yeah, that's what my dad says too. He's a right grumpy old bastard when he's on nights."

"Did you hear about Ian?"

Johnno nodded. "Yeah, it were in the local paper, it said he took a right fucking beating. How is he?"

"Still unconscious. You heard anything about who did it?" Trog glanced at the student punk and his mates. They glared back.

Johnno shook his head. "No, mate. But if you find out, let me know and I'll help you sort the bastard out. He were a good bloke, Ian."

"He still is," Trog said.

* * *

"Fucking hell Stiggy, you can't do that on here," Colin said when he saw Stiggy pull out a can of glue.

Stiggy shrugged. "Why not?"

"Because it will fucking stink," Brian said, "and the train guard will chuck us all off."

"Yeah well," Stiggy said, "not if I open a window it won't."

"Can't you do it in the bogs or something?"

"Nah, fuck that. I'm sick of hiding away, it's not like it's illegal or nothing." Stiggy unscrewed the lid and poured a blob of glue into a bag.

Brian frowned. "Yeah, well, you can fuck off to the other side of the carriage with it. And when the train guard catches you we don't know who you are, right?"

Stiggy shrugged and rose to his feet. He walked along the carriage to the exit door and pulled down its window. He leaned out, turned his head to face away from the wind, and raised the glue-bag to his mouth.

"Fucking dick," Brian said, shaking his head. Colin turned to watch Stiggy.

Stiggy let out a roar and leaned out further. He stretched up on his toes and shuffled his stomach across the window edge, then roared again. He raised his arms out sideways as if they were wings, and the glue-bag flew out of his hand. Then his feet rose from the ground and he started to tip out.

"Fucking hell," Colin shouted, jumping to his feet. He ran to the door and grabbed one of Stiggy's ankles. He could feel something hard in Stiggy's sock, but didn't have time to think what it might be. Stiggy's other leg kicked out wildly at him, narrowly missing his face. Colin yanked his foot, trying to pull Stiggy back inside the train. Stiggy clamped his hands against the outside of the train to stop him.

Brian rushed forward and took hold of Stiggy's other foot. They both tugged, fighting against Stiggy's apparent desire to jump out of the train. With both of them pulling together, Stiggy's hands began to slip. He roared in anger as he inched back inside, then let go and fell face down on the floor of the train.

Colin bent down and lifted up the bottom of Stiggy's combat trousers to see what was hidden in his sock. It was a knife with a vicious looking six inch blade, fastened to Stiggy's ankle with black masking tape.

"Fucking hell Bri, look at this!"

Brian's eyes widened when he looked at the knife. "Jesus fucking Christ. I told you that cunt was trouble. What the fuck's he doing with something like that?"

"Help me get it off," Colin said, pulling at the masking tape.

Between them they were able to remove enough of the tape to twist the knife loose.

"Oi that's mine," Stiggy yelled, and made a grab for the knife. Colin tossed it out of the train window. Stiggy made straight for the window, as if he was about to jump out after it. Brian grabbed his arms and held him back. Colin closed the window.

"What the fuck did you do that for?" Stiggy yelled. He struggled in Brian's grip.

"Why do you fucking think, you mad bastard," Brian said. "You can't take a fucking knife to a gig. What were you going to do, fucking stab a skinhead or what?"

"What's going on here?" A voice thundered from nearby.

Colin spun toward it. A six-foot, well built man of African descent wearing a train guard uniform glared at him.

"Nothing," Colin said. "Um ... he's not feeling very well. Travel sickness, you know."

"So why are you holding his arms like that then?" The train guard looked at Brian. Brian let go of Stiggy and shrugged. "Well?"

Brian glanced at Colin, then looked at the train guard. "Um... so he doesn't fall over? He got a bit dizzy."

"Is that right?" the train guard asked Stiggy.

Stiggy shrugged and glared at Colin. "Yeah," he said.

The train guard grunted. "Right, okay. Let me see your tickets." They presented their train tickets and he punched holes in them with a clipper. "Right. Now go and sit down, you're blocking the gangway here. And no more trouble or you'll be off the train at the next station. Clear?" They all nodded. The guard stood to one side and gestured for them to pass.

Colin and Brian sat down in the nearest vacant seat. Stiggy walked to the opposite end of the carriage, where he remained for the rest of the journey to Shefferham.

* * *

Colin squinted up at one of the seemingly endless blocks of high-rise flats that comprised Shefferham's landscape. He shielded his eyes from the sun and tried to imagine what it would be like to live so high up in the sky.

"So where do we go now?" Brian asked.

Twiglet pulled a crumpled piece of paper from his back pocket and unfolded it. "The Maples, Fitzholme Street," he read out loud.

"Where the fuck's that?" Colin asked.

"How should I know?" Twiglet said with a shrug.

Spazzo sighed. "You cunts are fucking useless. I knew I should have gone with Johnno instead."

"Yeah, right," Stiggy said with a sneer. "And them fucking skinheads he's mates with. So what's that about then?"

Spazzo shrugged. "Dunno. Johnno seems to know them from somewhere."

"Yeah well, anyone who hangs around with skinheads is a fucking cunt as far as I'm concerned."

"Yeah, I'd go along with that," Colin said, nodding. He saw an old woman across the road and called out to her. "Scuse us, missus." The old woman looked, then hurried on. Colin ran across the road to intercept her. "Scuse us, missus," he repeated.

"I haven't got no money," the old woman said. She stopped and raised her palms to Colin. Her hands shook as she stared at him wide-eyed.

"Neither have I," Colin said. "Do you know where there's a place called The Maples?"

"Never heard of it," she said, and turned and walked away.

"Hold up, missus. Oi Twiglet, what's the name of that road again?"

"Fitzholme Street," Twiglet shouted.

Colin caught up with the old woman and stood before her. "Scuse us, missus. Do you know where Fitzholme Street is?"

"Oh heck, you're miles off," she said, pointing back the way they had come. "It's up that way, about a mile or so past the train station."

Colin sighed. "Cheers, missus," he said. "We're going the wrong fucking way," he shouted to the others.

* * *

After asking a few more people for directions along the way, they arrived at Fitzholme Street a little under forty minutes later to join the end of a lopsided queue trailing down the outside of The Maples.

Stiggy glared at a group of twelve skinheads in front of them, and Colin saw his fists were clenched. He hoped Stiggy wouldn't start anything because they were vastly outnumbered. One of the skinheads, heavily built and standing a good six inches taller than the others, looked to be in his mid-twenties. He had his arm draped around the shoulder of a small, much younger girl with a shaved head and a long pink fringe. The other skinheads, all male, were closer to the girl's age than his, and he ordered one of them to go to the front of the queue and see what the hold-up was.

"There's a pair of fucking gorillas on the door," the young skinhead said when he returned. "They're searching every cunt that goes in."

Colin looked at Stiggy, wondering if he had any more weapons hidden away.

When they neared the front of the queue, Colin saw two black bouncers. They both had short cropped hair and were dressed in identical grey suits, both sporting a pair of dark sunglasses and the same scowl on their faces. People were let through the door one at a time and frisked. Confiscated items lay in a pile by the side of the door, mostly studded wristbands and bullet-belts, though Colin did see at least one knife glittering amongst them.

When it was the large skinhead's turn he raised his arms and glared at the two bouncers. One of the young skinheads, the next in line, started making monkey sounds. The bouncers waved the large skinhead through and beckoned for the younger skinhead to enter. He walked toward them swinging his arms from side to side. Grinning, he stood before the bouncers and raised his arms. One frisked him from behind while the other stood before him, glaring down. When the skinhead had been searched, the bouncer in front raised his foot and stamped down on his toes.

"Ah, you cunt," the skinhead cried, hopping on one leg. "What did you do that for?"

The bouncer shrugged. "Testing for steel toe caps. Now on your way, you little shit."

When they searched Stiggy one of the bouncers found his can of glue and tossed it at the pile of confiscated items. It landed on the tiled floor with a dull thud and rolled to a halt near an expensive-looking cassette recorder. Stiggy made as if to retrieve it, but the bouncer blocked his way.

"You can pick it up on your way out," the bouncer said. "Either now or at closing time, I don't care which."

Stiggy stood his ground. He stared at the bouncer and clenched his fists. The bouncer stared back, unfazed.

"Hurry up mate, we want to get in before the band comes on," a young punk standing behind Colin said.

"Yeah come on, Stiggy," Colin said. "You won't need it in there anyway, you can pick it up when we leave."

Stiggy held the bouncer's stare a moment longer before turning away. He looked at his glue, then turned back to the bouncer. "It had better be there when I come back out. And I know how much is in it too, so don't think about pinching any."

The bouncer laughed humourlessly and shook his head. "On your way, freak."

* * *

After they were all let into the venue Colin and Brian made straight for the bar, while the others took ownership of a table nearby. Spazzo procured an extra stool from the adjacent table, and they all shuffled closer together to make room for Colin and Brian when they returned with the drinks.

"Here you go Stiggy," Colin said, putting a pint of cider down before him. He sat down opposite and took a drink of his bitter.

Stiggy was staring at something over Colin's shoulder. Colin turned to look, and saw the group of skinheads standing at the bar. Several had taken off their flight jackets, revealing British Movement and Skrewdriver T-shirts beneath. The large, older skinhead pulled off his shirt and stuffed it down the back of his jeans, then faced outwards with his elbows leaning on the bar. His muscular chest and arms were covered in multi-coloured tattoos. The younger skinheads faced him reverently, pints of lager in their hands, while the skinhead girl stood to one side sipping from a bottle of Babycham.

"What the fuck sort of cider's this?" Stiggy said.

Colin turned back to Stiggy and watched him put down his glass and grimace. He shrugged. "I don't know. The cider sort, probably. Why, what's up with it?"

"Nowt. I suppose it'll have to do, won't it? You think me glue will be all right out there? There's fucking two quid's worth in that can, someone might nick it."

"Nah, who'd want that fucking shite?" Brian said. "I wouldn't mind that cassette recorder though if we're out first. Got to be worth a fucking hundred quid at least."

"I could do with a new cassette player meself," Colin said, nodding. "Me old one's broke."

Over the next half hour the venue started to fill up with an even mixture of punks and skinheads, plus a few nondescript youths in casual jeans and sweatshirts. The mob of skinheads at the bar were getting louder the more they drank. They kept looking over at Twiglet and nudging each other, then laughing. One pretended to be a monkey and they laughed louder.

Twiglet stared back at them, his arms folded. "Fucking Nazis," he said under his breath. "So proud of their white skin they cover it up with tattoos."

Brian laughed. "Yeah. Here's one for you. A skinhead walks into a bar. 'Ow,' he says."

"You what?" Twiglet asked, looking at Brian.

Brian smiled. "They lowered the entrance bar, didn't they?"

Twiglet shook his head and frowned. "What the fuck are you on about?"

"It was an *iron* bar, but it was okay because it only hit him on the head so no damage was done."

Colin snorted. Twiglet sighed and shook his head. He turned back to look at the skinheads.

"You know what, Bri?" Colin said, smiling. "That was a fucking shite joke, your worst yet."

Brian shrugged. "Yeah well, I only just thought of it so it probably needs a bit of work."

"It needs a fucking lot of work if you ask me. Or better yet, just never tell it again."

"All right, what about this one then? See that skinhead bird with the Babycham?" Colin looked and nodded. "It's Baby-Sham69, innit? The skinhead version, as drunk by Jimmy Pursey when he were a baby.

Colin smiled. "Singing If the Babies are United."

"There's Gonna Be A Nursery Breakout," Brian said.

"Hurry Up Mummy."

"Red Nappy Rash."

"You what?" Colin asked. "Which one's that then?"

"You know, Red London. It was their first single."

Colin shrugged. "Don't think I ever heard that one." He turned to Stiggy, who was staring at the skinhead girl. "What do you reckon Stiggy?"

Stiggy smiled when he caught the girl's eye. The girl glanced quickly at the group of skinheads, who were busy throwing beer mats at each other, and smiled back before turning her back on him.

"You what?" Stiggy said.

"Do you know any Baby-Sham69 songs?"

Stiggy shrugged, still staring at the skinhead girl. "No, not really."

* * *

The support group were a local punk band who introduced themselves as The Burglars.

"Smash the state!" the singer shouted, and an out-of-tune guitar started up. The guitarist stood with his back to the audience, as if he was embarrassed to be there. Bass and drums followed, and the singer launched himself into the song. He gripped the microphone stand in both hands and shook it angrily as he sang about how much he wanted to kill Thatcher.

The short song ended to complete silence from the audience. "Clap, you fuckers!" the singer shouted.

The skinheads at the bar started a slow hand clap, but nobody else joined in. The band started their next number, a cover version of an Exploited song that didn't quite sound right with a Yorkshire accent.

"Off, off, off," the skinheads chanted, punching the air.

Stiggy drained his glass and went to the bar. He stood next to the skinhead girl and shouted his order to the barman. She looked at the bare-chested skinhead, then turned away from the band to face the same direction as Stiggy. She leaned against the bar and took a sip of Babycham. Stiggy looked at her and smiled, then said something into her ear. She smiled back and looked away.

The band on stage continued to play, despite an obviously hostile audience who just wanted them to hurry up and finish.

* * *

"All roight?" Manny's amplified voice yelled from the stage.

A swarm of punks and skinheads rushed forward as one. One hand on the microphone, Manny glared down at the expectant faces of the crowd.

"We're all fucking upstarts!" he shouted, and everyone roared their approval, drowning out the opening guitar intro. A drum roll started the song proper, and Manny screamed out the words. A punk climbed onto the stage, and before the two bouncers could react he dived back into the audience. The area immediately in front of the stage was soon full of jerking bodies jostling for position.

"They tell us what to think, they tell us who to see," Manny growled in his rough, guttural cockney voice. He picked up the microphone stand and swung it down into the crowd.

Dozens of hands made a grab for it.

"We're all upstarts, you and me!" everyone in the audience screamed.

Manny yanked the microphone stand away from them and held it aloft above his head before slamming it back down on the stage. He picked up a can of beer while the band continued playing, and shook it furiously. He aimed the can at the audience and pulled the ring-pull, showering the front row with beer. He poured the remaining beer over his own head and crushed the empty can in his hand before drop-kicking it away.

A young skinhead barged Colin in the shoulder. Colin barged him back, grinning, and sent him stumbling away. Nearby, Brian spun his arms around like a double sided windmill, clearing out his own little space within the melee as people scrambled to avoid him. Twiglet and Spazzo were right at the front of the stage together, pressed up tight by the surging crowd behind them, so only their upper bodies could jerk in time to the music.

The song ended with a final scream from Manny and the crowd stopped its gyrations as one. Colin lifted up his T-shirt and wiped sweat from his face. He turned to speak to Brian, but Brian was too far away, surrounded by skinheads. He looked for Stiggy, but couldn't see him anywhere.

The band started their second song, and the dancing resumed. The young skinhead rushed toward Colin again, his right elbow pointing outwards like a lance, his hand clamped behind his neck. He had a wide, lop-sided grin on his face.

Colin dodged to one side just before the skinhead reached him, and gave him a quick shove in the back as he hurtled past. He soared into the back of a punk, who lost his balance and went down. The skinhead tripped over him and landed on top of the punk in a pile of flailing arms and legs.

Colin's energy started to flag after a few more songs. When Manny started on one of his between-song monologues about police oppression he saw it as an opportunity for a quick rest break and a gulp of beer. Manny was telling a story about a time when he was arrested and beaten up in the cells by a policeman who objected to the 'Who Killed Liddle?' T-shirt he wore. It was a story Colin already knew from an interview with Manny he had read in Sounds several months earlier, so he weaved his way out of the crowd and made for the table where he had left his beer. Punks and skinheads parted before him, then fought over the space he had vacated.

Colin slumped into his seat and took a long drink. Over the rim of his glass he saw Stiggy leaning against the now deserted bar, watching the band with the skinhead girl. Stiggy's left arm rested on the bar, behind the skinhead girl's shoulder as she took casual sips from her Babycham bottle.

Colin sighed and shook his head. He tried to get Stiggy's attention, but Stiggy either didn't hear him or chose not to. Instead, he started drawing little circles on the skinhead girl's shoulder with his fingertip. She turned to face him and they stared into each other's eyes for a few seconds. She looked toward the stage area, then leaned her head into Stiggy's chest. Stiggy closed his arm around her.

Colin gaped at them open mouthed, not believing what he was seeing. He looked across at the stage area, expecting to see hordes of outraged skinheads tearing toward him. But the band had started playing again, and everyone was too busy leaping around to notice anything else.

Colin's hands shook as he drank the rest of his beer. This was bad. Very bad. He had to get Stiggy out of there before the skinheads saw him messing with their bird. But he couldn't do it on his own, he would need help. Maybe Brian could shout some sense into Stiggy, and if that didn't work they would all just have to drag him away from her by force.

Colin returned to the stage area, but he couldn't see Brian anywhere for all the jerking, spasmodic bodies leaping around. He inched his way through the crowd to where he had seen him last, prising people apart to make a gap big enough to squeeze through. Some parted easily, others resisted and he needed to physically barge past them. A few, unwilling to give up their position under any circumstances, turned and pushed him in the chest, sending him stumbling back a few steps, further away from his goal.

Colin didn't make much headway into the heart of the crowd until a song ended and the audience started to relax and thin out to avoid the body heat given off by their closest neighbours. Pushing his way through, he found Brian just as the next song started, and his shouted words were drowned out by a crashing wall of sound from the nearby PA system.

Colin pulled on Brian's arm to get him out of the crowd so he could talk to him properly, but Brian must have thought he wanted to dance because he grabbed a handful of Colin's shirt and swung him around by it. The unexpected momentum took Colin by surprise and he was propelled into the back of a stocky skinhead. The skinhead turned and pushed Colin away. Colin stumbled back and lost his balance, then tumbled to the ground.

Two arms came down to help Colin back to his feet. When he looked up he saw it was the same skinhead who had been barging him earlier, the same lop-sided grin on his face. The skinhead pulled Colin to his feet and looped a sweaty arm around his neck. He rushed into the crowd, pulling Colin with him.

Surrounded by writhing bodies packed closely together, Colin had no option but to wait until the next lull between songs. He hoped it would last long enough for him to reach Brian and warn him about what was going to happen.

The song ended, but there was no rest gap, no opportunity to reach Brian.

"Police Scum!" Manny shouted, and the band immediately started playing again. This was the song Cockney Upstarts usually ended their set with, so Colin knew he didn't have much time left. People at the back of the crowd surged forward, causing even more of a crush around the stage.

Manny pulled the microphone from its stand and screamed into it. He raised his arms above his head and launched himself from the stage like an Olympic diver. Twenty pairs of arms rose to catch him and lower him to the ground. Manny was in the midst of the crowd, singing Police Scum, everyone within range of the microphone shouting along with him. Those just out of range fought for a closer position.

Colin was swept along by the crowd as everyone clawed their way closer to Manny, all wanting to be a part of the band for their anthem title. Someone wrenched the microphone from Manny's hand, and his voice was replaced with a gruff Yorkshire accent that screamed the words out of tune. Manny lost his footing and fell when the crowd around him surged after the microphone. He raised his arms to protect his head as boots swarmed over him, oblivious to his plight.

The song ended, and the band stopped playing, but the crowd around the microphone continued singing, starting up a rendition of We're All Upstarts. The lead guitarist and bass player jumped off the stage and pulled Manny to his feet. Blood poured from his nose and mouth as they led him away.

The crowd started to thin out as people drifted away to the bar for one final drink before they made their way home. The skinheads were busy giving Nazi salutes and sieg heiling to each other. Colin saw his chance to get to Brian.

***

"Stiggy's off on one again, we need to get him out of here quick."

Brian rolled his eyes and nodded. "I told you we shouldn't have fetched him." He sighed and beckoned Twiglet and Spazzo over. They both had red faces and were dripping with sweat.

"Fucking smart or what?" Twiglet said. His smile dropped when he looked at Colin's concerned expression. "What's up?"

"Fucking Stiggy," Colin said. "He's that fucking glued up he's chatting up a skinhead bird at the bar." He pointed at the group of skinheads by the stage, who seemed to have had their fill of Nazi salutes and were jumping on each other's shoulders. "We need to get him out of here before that lot find out."

Stiggy looked like he was about to leave when they reached him. He stood by the bar, holding hands with the skinhead girl, and they turned toward the exit together.

"Stiggy wait," Colin shouted.

Stiggy looked over his shoulder but continued walking.

"Oi, that's my fucking bird, you cunt!" someone shouted from nearby.

Colin spun around. The bare-chested skinhead ran straight at him, followed by his young mates. Colin's stomach flipped. This was it, Stiggy was toast and there was nothing he could do about it. They were too late. Colin stepped to one side as the skinheads thundered past.

The barman disappeared through a door into a back room. Colin looked for the two bouncers, and saw them standing guard at the band's dressing room door. They were smiling as they watched, arms folded across their chests.

"Leave him, Joe," the skinhead girl said. She stood between Stiggy and the large skinhead, looking tiny and frail in comparison. Her bottom lip trembled as she clenched her fists by her sides.

"Get out of the fucking way," the skinhead snarled. He lunged forward and slapped her in the face with the back of his hand.

She staggered back, her hand rising to a bright red mark on her face where she had been struck. She stumbled and Stiggy caught her in his arms. The skinhead stepped up to her and punched her in the stomach. She doubled over and fell to her knees groaning.

Stiggy roared and ran at the skinhead. He picked up an empty Babycham bottle from the bar and raised it, then swung it down at the skinhead's head. The skinhead brought up one of his tattoo-covered arms just in time, and the bottle thudded into it. He grabbed Stiggy's wrist and twisted it. Stiggy cried out and dropped the bottle. The skinhead stamped down on it, shattering it beneath his boot, and wrenched Stiggy's arm up his back. Stiggy bent over, yelling. The skinhead roared and shoved him head-first into the bar. Stiggy crumpled to the ground and the skinhead moved in for the kill. Stiggy curled himself up into a ball while the skinhead kicked out at his arms and legs. The young skinheads cheered him on.

Twiglet and Spazzo rushed forward to intercept. The young skinheads swarmed over them and they went down in a hail of fists and boots. Brian jumped on the large skinhead's back and wrapped his arms around his neck. He kicked out his legs to unbalance him. The skinhead twisted and turned, trying to punch Brian in the face. The girl stumbled up to Stiggy, holding her stomach with one hand.

Colin knew he should do something to help Brian but he was frozen to the spot. He watched the skinhead girl help Stiggy to his feet, then support him with an arm around his waist while they staggered to the exit together. It was only when the group of young skinheads got bored of kicking the unconscious bodies of Twiglet and Spazzo and looked around for a fresh target that he sprang into action.

Colin rushed up to the large skinhead and pushed him in the chest with both hands. He toppled over, Brian still clinging to his back. Brian gave out a loud gasp when the skinhead landed on top of him. His hands fell to his sides. The skinhead rolled over and straddled him, then raised his fists to pummel his upturned face.

Colin grabbed the skinhead around the neck and pulled with all his might. The skinhead sprang up and spun to face him. He laughed and grabbed Colin's wrists, stretched his arms out wide and pulled Colin closer. His head snapped back, then launched forward to smack Colin on the bridge of his nose.

Blinding pain soared through Colin. The skinhead pushed him away, into the waiting arms of the younger skinheads, who pulled him to the ground and went to work on him with their boots.

* * *

Trog watched the scuffle at the bar with interest. It wasn't his fight, so there was no need to get involved. The gobby student punk and his mates were getting a right fucking hammering though. The Shefferham mob had no class the way they were all steaming in six onto one. Trog preferred a fair fight, something you could brag about to your mates later. This was just the sort of brutal thuggery that gave skinheads a bad name.

Someone yelled "Coppers!" and everyone drew silent to listen. Trog heard two-tone sirens wailing in the distance, until a mass stampede for the exit door drowned them out.

"Time to get fucked off," Don said. Trog nodded and followed him to the exit.

Near the bar, the tattooed skinhead picked up the stem of a broken Babycham bottle and straddled the gobby student's mate. He smiled as he raised the jagged glass shard above his head like a dagger. Trog stopped to watch, torn between intervening and getting the fuck out of there while he still had time.

The gobby student's mate cried out and raised his hands to protect his face. The skinhead slashed down and sliced through a wrist. Blood spurted like it had been shot from a water pistol and splattered over the skinhead's chest.

"Trog, come on," Don yelled, "we need to get fucked off before the coppers get here."

"You go on, I'll catch you up later. Meet me at the train station if you need to scarper from outside."

Trog ran up to the skinhead just as he raised the broken bottle again. He made a grab for his wrist, but the skinhead jerked it away at the last second and backhanded Trog across the face. Trog stumbled back. The skinhead laughed and rammed the broken bottle into the punk's neck. He pulled it out and threw it at Trog, then swaggered casually toward the exit door.

* * *

Colin opened his eyes and groaned. Every inch of his body ached. Sirens howled in the distance, getting closer. Colin rolled onto his side and pushed himself up onto his knees. He shook his head and looked around. Tables and chairs were tipped over. Broken glass littered the floor. Twiglet lay groaning a few feet away. Spazzo sat holding his face in his hands, blood dripping between his fingers.

Colin looked down when he realised his knees were wet, and saw a large pool of blood. He searched his body frantically for knife wounds. When he found none he looked behind him and gasped. Brian lay still on the ground, a skinhead straddled over him.

Hands around Brian's neck.

Strangling him.

Rage surged through Colin. It was the same skinhead who had been giving him hassle all week, the midget bald bastard who had attacked him for no reason in The Queen's Head. And now he was killing Brian.

"You've had it now, you fucking cunt!" Colin roared. He ran at the skinhead, adrenalin coursing through his body and giving strength to his aching limbs. He barrelled into him, hands outstretched, and pushed him off Brian. The skinhead rolled onto his side and sat up, glaring at Colin. Blood spurted from a large, gaping wound in Brian's neck. Colin stared in shock. Brian was unconscious, his face deathly white.

The skinhead crawled back to Brian and clamped a hand over his neck. "We need to put pressure on the wounds or he'll fucking bleed to death," he said.

Colin gaped, open mouthed. The skinhead looked up at him. "For fuck's sake, get down here and help me or he'll fucking die!"

Colin knelt down and stared at Brian, saw more blood gushing from his wrist. "What do I do?"

"Take your belt off and tie it around his arm, just below the elbow. As tight as you can. Then hold his arm up. I hope that's a fucking ambulance I can hear coming."

Colin removed his belt and held it out to the skinhead. "I don't know what to do. You should do it, you seem to know what you're doing."

The skinhead glared at him. "If I let go of his neck again he'll fucking die. Now fucking do it or I'll fucking batter you! Get that fucking belt round his fucking arm! Now!" Colin startled, almost dropping the belt. "For fuck's sake, just do it you useless cunt!"

Colin looped the belt around Brian's arm and pushed the end through the buckle. "Here?" he asked, still unsure if this was the right thing to do or not.

"A bit further up his arm," the skinhead said. Colin slid the belt a few inches closer to Brian's elbow. "That's it. Now pull the fucker tight and don't let go."

Colin looked at the jagged gash in Brian's wrist while he pulled the belt tighter. The gushing blood slowed to a trickle.

"It's working," Colin said, amazed. "Shouldn't we do the same with his neck?"

The skinhead looked up and shook his head slowly. "Don't be fucking daft."

"But ..."

Before Colin could finish his sentence, police swarmed through the door with a loud yell. Colin looked up just in time to see a raised truncheon hurtle toward his face, then he slumped over Brian and lost consciousness.

6 Police Bastard

The ground vibrated beneath Colin's cheek. He lifted his head and opened his eyes, saw a row of boots and trainers before him. The ground fell away, then jerked up to smack him in the face. He groaned and sat up, rubbing his sore head. Battered, bleeding faces stared down at him. The police van drove over another pot-hole, jarring his aching spine.

"You, sit down with the other scum," someone shouted.

Colin turned his head slowly, every movement causing intense pain. A policeman glared at him, tapping a truncheon into the palm of his hand.

"You all right, Col?" Spazzo asked. He reached down and helped Colin to his feet. The van lurched around a corner. Colin stumbled and fell against the other punks lining the wall of the van. A few swore at him, others reached out to help him regain his balance and sit down on the bench.

Colin looked at the faces staring at him from another bench at the opposite side of the van. The skinhead who had been helping Brian nodded to him. Blood dripped from a gash in the side of his head, his face a mass of bruises.

Colin startled. "Where's Brian?" he asked, searching the faces of the other occupants of the van.

"No talking," the policeman shouted.

The skinhead shrugged. "I don't know, mate. Hopefully down at the hospital."

"Is he all right? Did we save him?"

The policeman tapped the truncheon into the palm of his hand with more force. "I said no fucking talking!"

Trog shook his head and looked down at his boots. "I don't know, mate. I held on as long as I could but there was too many fucking coppers and they battered me the same way they battered you. I don't know what happened after that, it's not long since I came round meself."

* * *

"Empty your pockets on the desk and remove your belt and shoe laces."

A broad-shouldered, overweight policeman in his late forties glared at Colin from behind a counter. He picked up a cracked mug and took a loud slurp from its contents.

"Is there any news about me mate?" Colin asked.

The policeman scowled. "What mate would that be?"

"He got stabbed. We were trying to help him."

The policeman shrugged. "Don't know, don't care. Now empty your pockets and remove your belt and shoe laces."

Colin crouched down and removed the laces from his trainers, then put them on the counter.

"And the belt," the policeman said.

Colin lifted his T-shirt. "I haven't got one, it's on me mate's arm."

The policeman grunted. "Empty your pockets."

Colin rifled through his pockets in turn, and put the contents on the desk. The policeman poked through them with a pen, separating them out. He picked up Colin's cigarettes and put them in his pocket.

"These will need testing for drugs," he said, glaring at Colin. "You got any objections to that?"

Colin shook his head. The policeman pulled out a form and wrote down an itemised list of Colin's remaining possessions. He spoke aloud as he put them in a plastic bag.

"One handkerchief, used. One train ticket, used." The policeman counted out Colin's loose change and dropped it into the bag. "Seventy-six pence in coins. One cigarette lighter. One wallet." He picked up Colin's wallet, flipped it open, and took out a five pound note and two one pound notes. He looked Colin in the eye and continued his inventory. "One wallet, empty."

Colin took a step closer to the counter. "What? Oh come on, I need that for the train home."

"One wallet, *empty*," the policeman repeated.

Colin looked down at his feet. "Fucking bastard," he said under his breath.

"What was that?" the policeman asked, leaning forward and scowling.

Colin shook his head. "Nothing."

The policeman sealed the plastic bag and pushed the form across the counter to Colin. "Sign here," he said and dropped the pen on top of the form.

Colin signed his name at the bottom of the form and put the pen down. "So what happens now?" he asked.

"We'll get you checked over by a doctor, then you can go to beddy-byes in the cells. You'll be processed in the morning with the others."

"What? I can't stay here all night, me Gran will be worried if I don't come home."

The policeman sighed. "You're entitled to one phone call, you can use that to let her know what a naughty boy you've been."

Colin frowned. "We're not on the phone."

The policeman shrugged. "Well she'll just have to worry then, won't she?"

* * *

The doctor gave Colin a cursory examination, then declared him fit enough for custody. A policeman led Colin by the arm to a cell and pushed him inside. The door slammed behind Colin and he spun to face it. An observation hatch slid open. A face scowled through it for a few seconds, then the hatch slid shut.

Colin looked around the small cell. A bed, little more than a wooden shelf jutting out of one wall, had a thin rubber mattress on top to sleep on. There were no sheets or pillows, and the mattress itself had dark stains on it that Colin didn't want to think about. The cell smelled of faeces, the stench coming from a chipped porcelain toilet in one corner. It had no seat, and overflowed with foul-looking waste.

Someone in the next cell sang out of tune, slurring his words. The man's voice rose and fell in volume, occasionally punctuated by a belch.

"Shut it," someone shouted. The off-key singing became louder. Colin heard footsteps outside, and the scrape of an observation hatch sliding open. "I said shut it, you fucking black bastard."

The drunken singer stopped in mid-line, only to resume again from where he left off when the hatch was closed.

Keys jangled, a lock opened, and a door slammed back on its hinges. Colin heard a short scuffle, followed by a cry of pain. The door slammed again, and heavy footsteps clumped toward Colin's own cell. His observation hatch opened. A face scowled in through the rectangular opening. Colin looked at the man and held his hands up in surrender. The hatch closed.

"Wait," Colin shouted, walking up to the door. "Is there any news about me mate? He got stabbed at The Maples earlier tonight."

The scowling face reappeared and glared in at him. His mouth turned into a sneer. "Died on the way to the hospital," he said. "Good fucking riddance if you ask me. One less scumbag on the streets for us to deal with."

Colin's world lurched to one side. Blood rushed to his head, an ice-cold shiver ran down his spine. He staggered across to the bed and slumped down on it, holding his face in his hands. He cried for the first time in twelve years, his body shaking with loud, uncontrollable sobs.

* * *

The next day, Colin was fingerprinted and then released without charge.

"A witness backed up your version of the story," he was told by a scowling police officer.

Colin didn't really care. None of that mattered any more. His best mate, someone he had grown up with and had known most of his life, was dead. Murdered by a skinhead he didn't even know, over something he didn't even have anything to do with.

Colin fought back the tears as he was given back his possessions and signed a form to confirm they were all present and correct. He did this without question. The loss of his cigarettes and money just didn't seem important any more. He didn't even notice his cigarette lighter was also missing.

Stepping out into the glaring sun, Colin saw the short skinhead sitting on a wall outside the police station. The skinhead jumped down and walked toward him.

"What did they do you for?" he asked.

"Nothing," Colin said, looking down at the skinhead's boots.

"Jammy bastard. They did me for affray and resisting arrest. Fucking cunts, all I were doing was trying to keep your mate alive until the ambulances got there."

"Brian's dead," Colin said. His voice came out as a squeak, and a tear rolled down his cheek.

The skinhead looked at him in silence for a few seconds, then shook his head. "Mate, that's a fucking shame. I know we had our differences, but fucking hell. No cunt deserves to die like that."

Colin sniffed and wiped his nose on the back of his hand.

"You know ..." the skinhead began, then looked away. "I ... er ... I'm sorry I whacked you the other night. You caught me at a bad time. I'd just split up with me bird, you see, and –"

"It doesn't really matter now, does it?"

"I'm Trog," the skinhead said, holding out his hand. When Colin didn't take it, he lowered it to his side. "Have you got any money? Some bastard copper took all mine, and I haven't got enough for the train. I can pay you back double when we get home, I'll get me brother to meet us at the train station."

"No," Colin said, shaking his head. "They took all my money as well, I've only got about sixty pence left. Fuck. How are we going to get home?"

Trog frowned. "Bollocks, I was hoping it were just me. I've only got about thirty pence meself. Never mind, I've got another idea. Come on."

* * *

At the train station, Colin waited outside a telephone box while Trog called his brother.

"All sorted," Trog said when he stepped out.

"You think it will work?" Colin asked.

"Yeah, no worries. Besides, have you got any better ideas?" Colin shook his head. "Well come on then. Trust me."

They bought a platform ticket each and passed through the barrier onto the platform. Colin bought a pack of ten cigarettes from a kiosk and begged a light from a passing woman. It was the first cigarette he had smoked since the previous night, and on an empty stomach the nicotine rush made him light headed.

When the train arrived they boarded it and headed straight for the toilet in the end carriage. Trog put the toilet lid down and sat on it. Colin squeezed in by a small sink opposite the toilet and closed the door behind him. He was about to lock it when Trog stopped him.

"Don't lock the door."

"Why not?" Colin's hand hovered over the lock, ready to slide it into place.

"The conductor will know there's someone in here if you lock it, and he'll wait outside to check our tickets. If he sees it unlocked he'll think it's empty and just walk past."

"But what if someone comes in?" Colin asked.

"Stick your foot against the door, they'll think it's jammed."

Colin sat down on the floor with his back against the door. He pulled out his cigarettes, but Trog told him to put them away. Colin frowned, remembering he didn't have anything to light them with anyway, and put the cigarettes back in his pocket.

"So how did you know what to do?" he asked.

Trog shrugged. "I used to do it all the time when I were a kid."

Colin looked up and shook his head. "No, I mean with Brian. That stuff you were doing, and that thing with the belt and all that."

"Learned it at work, didn't I?"

"Work?" Colin asked. His eyes widened. He didn't know anyone his age who had a job, and this revelation came as a complete surprise to him.

"Yeah."

"What are you, like a doctor or something?"

Trog laughed. "Nah, I work down the pit. I'm training to be a deputy. I wanted to be an electrician really, but they didn't have any of them left when I applied, so I went for deputy instead. First aid is part of what a deputy does. You know, for when there's like an accident or something."

"What's it like down the pit? I nearly applied meself when I left school, but me Gran wouldn't let me."

Trog snorted. "It's a bit of a shit hole, but a job's a job innit? The money's good, and they'll always need miners so it's a job for life. It beats being on the fucking dole anyway. Half my mates are on the dole and they're always fucking skint."

* * *

Colin opened the toilet door a few inches when the train pulled into their station. He peered out to check the coast was clear before opening it fully. They left the train and headed for the waiting room, where Trog said he had arranged to meet his brother.

"Piece of fucking piss," Trog said, smiling. "We'll get the new platform tickets from me brother, then we're home free. Fucking literally."

Trog was still grinning right up until he pushed open the waiting room door. A bald, stocky man in his early fifties glared up at him from a seated position at the far end of the waiting room.

"Dad, what are you doing here?" Trog asked.

Trog's father lumbered toward him, a look of thunder in his eyes. "You stupid fucking cunt," he yelled, and struck Trog across the face with the back of his hand. "How many times do I need to tell you?" He punched Trog in the stomach. Trog doubled over, the man brought his knee up into Trog's face.

Colin stared at the man in shock as Trog fell onto his back. He didn't know if he should try to help Trog or not, whether he even could do anything against this monster if he wanted to. The man was about to launch a kick at Trog's prone body when he noticed Colin standing there. He wheeled toward him.

"And you," the man said, jabbing Colin in the chest with his finger. "You'd better stay away from Stephen from now on, or I'll fucking kill you. I'm not having cunts like you leading him astray. You got that?"

Colin nodded, backing away.

"Good. Now here's your fucking ticket, so fuck off. This is family business, nothing to do with you."

The man threw a platform ticket on the floor. Colin picked it up, his eyes staying on the older man the whole time. He backed out of the waiting room, watching as the man turned his attention back to his son and started yelling.

Colin made his way to the train station exit. His hand shook as he handed over the platform ticket to a guard standing by the barrier. The guard gave the ticket a cursory glance and tore it in half, then waved Colin through the barrier. Colin let out a sigh, not realising he had been holding his breath.

A man sat on a bench outside the train station, reading the local newspaper and smoking a cigarette. Colin approached him and asked for a light. The man looked up from his newspaper. His eyes widened when he took in Colin's battered appearance, but he nodded. He folded up the newspaper and put it down beside him on the bench, then reached into a pocket. He pulled out a lighter and handed it to Colin.

"Cheers mate," Colin said. He lit his cigarette and gave the man his lighter back. The man put it away and picked up the newspaper. Colin gaped at the front page headline when the man unfolded the newspaper. He snatched it from the man's hands so he could read it.

PUNK RIOT, LOCAL YOUTH CRITICAL!

Colin skimmed the story, looking for specific names and details. He smiled, then read the article again from the beginning, just to make sure.

A riot broke out at a Shefferham punk rock concert last night. "It was like something out of a cowboy film," said the head of security at pop music venue The Maples. Local punk rocker Brian Mathews, unemployed, was rushed to hospital following a stabbing incident during the riot. He is said to be in a stable but critical condition. "He was lucky the police were on hand to give first aid assistance," said a hospital spokesman. Several other punk rockers were also injured and required hospital treatment. The Star says: Do we really want this punk rock menace on the streets of Shefferham?

Colin held the newspaper out to its owner and grinned. "He's not dead. He's not fucking dead!"

The man edged away from Colin, palms raised. Colin

smiled at the man, and took a step toward him to give him his newspaper back, but the man turned and ran away. Colin shrugged and put the newspaper down on the bench.

All he had to do now was walk home and think of some excuse he could give his Gran for staying out all night. That and make sure she didn't see the local paper.

7 Life Moves On

Mike Thornton and Twiglet both frowned when Trog walked up to their table in The White Swan. He put down a tray containing two pints of bitter and a pint of lager, then sat down between Colin and Brian.

"Cheers Trog," Colin said. He lifted one of the glasses and took a long drink.

"Yeah, cheers," Brian said, nodding his head.

It was Brian's first night out since being discharged from hospital the previous week. He'd jumped at the chance to get out of the house when Colin called round for him earlier in the evening, especially when Colin said he had arranged to meet Becky and Kaz. Brian confided in Colin as they left that he was sick of his mother fussing over him all the time, like he was some sort of invalid. She made Colin swear he wouldn't let Brian drink any alcohol, and that he would keep him well away from any skinheads. She didn't believe Colin's story that it had been a skinhead who saved Brian's life, preferring to believe the newspaper version saying it had been the police who saved him.

"It should be me buying you one though, I reckon," Brian said, looking at Trog.

Trog held up his hand and waved off the offer. "Nah, don't worry about it. I got some good news today anyway."

"Oh yeah?" Colin said, leaning forward. "What's that then?"

"Ian finally woke up this afternoon, it looks like he's going to be okay."

"Lazy bastard," Mike said with a grin. Trog glared across the table at him. "What?" Mike asked with a shrug.

"He was in a fucking coma, you cunt."

"Ah, okay, sorry mate. So what were up with him, like? Car crash or something?"

"Some cunt twatted him on the way home a few weeks

ago."

Mike looked at Colin. Colin looked away.

"So, um," Mike said, "has he said who it was that smacked him then?"

Trog shook his head slowly, maintaining eye contact with Mike. "No, not yet. He says he can't remember anything, but the doctor says that's just temporary and it'll all come back to him over the next few weeks."

"I'm just off to the bog," Mike announced, and rose to his feet.

Trog watched him go, then turned to Colin. "So where's that scruffy mate of yours, Stinky or whatever his name is?"

"Stiggy? Fuck knows. I haven't seen him since the Cockney Upstarts gig. I went round to his flat the other week but he wasn't there. The Rasta next door said he hadn't seen him either."

"He's probably off his fucking head on glue somewhere," Brian said. "You know what he's like."

Colin shrugged. "Yeah, probably. I just wish he'd get in touch though. I nearly shit meself when I heard about that bloke they found in Shefferham with his head stoved in. I were sure that was Stiggy until they showed a photo of him on the news. I thought them fucking skinheads must have caught up with him or something." He looked at Trog. "No offence, like," he added.

"None taken," Trog said. "They weren't skinheads anyway, they were fucking boneheads."

"What's the difference?" Twiglet asked.

Trog looked at the half-caste in silence for a few seconds before replying. "Boneheads are fucking Nazis."

Twiglet snorted. "What, and skinheads aren't?"

"Nah, are they fuck."

Born to Run started playing on the pub's jukebox as Mike returned from the toilet and went to the bar. Twiglet groaned and shook his head. "Oh, fuck off!"

"No, straight up," Trog said. "Your proper skinheads don't give a fuck about all that Hitler bollocks. We love our country too much to worship some fucking German cunt. Anyway, I'm off." He turned to Brian and patted him on the back. "Good to see you out and about again, anyway. If you want to come down to The Black Bull later I'll introduce you to the rest of the lads."

Brian nodded. "Yeah, I might do one day. Not tonight though, I'm meeting me bird in here in a bit, then we're off down to The Juggler's Rest to see a band."

"Yeah?" Trog said, grinning. "Well give her one for me. And enjoy your fucking hippy music."

Twiglet and Mike were singing as Trog left. They raised their beer glasses and clashed them together.

"Scum like us, maybe we don't give a fu-uck!"

* * *

"Lager, Trog?"

"Yeah, cheers Mandy." Trog looked over at a group of skinheads and raised his hand to them.

"Good news about Ian," Mandy said as she pulled his lager.

"Yeah," Trog said, smiling. "He's gonna be fucking ugly for a while though, until they fix his face up. But the way them nurses are fussing over him he's loving every fucking minute of it."

Trog pulled out his wallet to pay for the drink. Mandy shook her head. "No, don't worry about it. This one's on me. So how did you get on in court the other day?"

"Fifty quid fine and thirty-six hours attendance centre."

"Attendance centre? What's that then?"

Trog shrugged. "Dunno, some new bollocks they've come up with. I have to go to this place in Shefferham every Saturday afternoon for the next ten weeks."

"Oh," Mandy said, looking down. "Do you have to go this weekend?"

"Yeah. They said if I miss any they'll add an extra five hours on top of the ones I miss, as well as another fine."

"That's a shame. There's a Ska festival on at Cleethorpes this weekend, I thought you might want to come with me? We could get a room in a bed and breakfast, my treat." She leaned her elbows on the bar and smiled across at him, her chin cradled in her hands.

Trog closed his eyes and ran his hand over the stubble on the back of his head. "I should really go to this attendance centre thing," he said, avoiding Mandy's gaze.

"You could go there next weekend instead, I'm sure they won't mind. Go on, it'll be fucking brilliant. I haven't been to anything like that for years. We wouldn't need to spend the whole weekend at the festival, there's other stuff we could do. And it'll be a right laugh, there'll be skins from all over the country there. It'll be just like the old days."

Trog frowned, then nodded his head. "Yeah, fuck it. They'll have to do without me this week. I'll tell them I'm sick or something."

Mandy jumped up and down, clapping her hands together, and squealed in excitement. She reached across the bar and grabbed Trog by the neck with both hands, pulled him close, and hugged him.

* * *

Colin, Brian, Becky and Kaz were in The Juggler's Rest watching the band set up their equipment when Stiggy walked through the door with a short-haired girl in a baggy Discharge T-shirt.

"Stiggy!" Colin shouted. "Where the fuck have you been? And what's with the fucking beard?"

Stiggy grinned and raised a hand. He went to the bar for drinks, then swaggered over to their table.

"All right, Col?" Stiggy said. "You remember Sally, right?"

Colin looked at the short-haired girl standing by Stiggy's

side.

"All right," she said, nodding.

It took Colin a while to recognise her at first, because she had cut off her pink fringe and the rest of her hair was starting to grow out. It was the bottle of Babycham in her hand that clinched it.

"Er, yeah. All right, Sally."

"I brung your record," Stiggy said. He reached into his jacket and pulled out a twelve inch album. "I thought it were shite at first, but it sort of grows on you after a while."

Colin took the record and flipped it over to look at the front cover. With everything that had happened he had forgot all about lending it to Stiggy.

"Cheers, Stiggy. So how did you know we'd be in here?"

Stiggy shrugged. "Friday, innit? Where else would you be?"

"So where have you been then?"

"Here and there."

Brian drained his glass and rose to his feet. "Anyone want anything from the bar?"

Kaz frowned. "Should you be drinking that much in your condition?"

Brian groaned. "Don't you start as well. I've had me mam fussing round me ever since I got out of hospital. I've only had a few pints, it's not like I'm going to get smashed out of my head and start a fight with a gang of skinheads." He looked at Stiggy. Stiggy's face reddened.

"Yeah well," Stiggy said. "That's all sorted now. We—" Sally looked sharply at Stiggy and nudged him in the ribs. Stiggy looked away and took a sip from his cider. He sat down opposite Colin and cradled the glass in his hand. "Look, the thing is, we're getting off in the morning. There's some people after us, so we're moving away."

"What, for good?" Colin asked.

"Yeah."

"Where are you going, like?" Brian asked.

Stiggy opened his mouth to speak, but Sally got in first. "Manchester."

Colin frowned. "What the fuck's in Manchester?"

Stiggy looked at Sally, then shrugged. "No idea, I've never been. But I reckon it's a big city with loads of people, so it'll be easy to lose ourselves there."

"Blimey," Brian said. "Fucking Manchester, eh? Well good luck with it, yeah?"

Stiggy nodded. "Cheers Brian. That means a lot."

"You'll keep in touch though?" Colin asked. "Send me your address when you get sorted so we can all come down and visit?"

"Yeah, of course I will," Stiggy said, looking away.

"So," Colin said, rising to his feet. He held his beer glass out in a toast. "Here's to Stiggy. Cunt of the year, 1982."

"Piss off," Stiggy said with a wide grin.

Printed in Great Britain
by Amazon